FEAR OF FALLING

SECRETS IN THE SNOW ~ BOOK 1

ROZ MARSHALL

Eden
Press

Find out more about the author and upcoming books online at www. rozmarshall.co.uk

Get **the series prequel FREE**—sign up for my newsletter:

rozmarshall.co.uk/welcome/

For 'Billy the Brush', a great family friend, who sadly died while I was working on this book

PLEASE NOTE

This book was previously published as Episode 2 of the series. This 2020 edition has been extensively rewritten and extended.

The previous book, *Winter Arrives*, which introduces the characters and tells the story of how Jude took over the ski school, can be obtained for free by signing up to my mailing list: rozmarshall.co.uk/welcome/

This is the series in chronological order:

- Winter Arrives
- Skiing with Santa
- A Dream for New Year
- Fear of Falling
- The Snow Patrol
- My Snowy Valentine

- The Racer Trials
- Snow Blind
- Weathering the Storm

ABOUT THIS BOOK

Fiona Easton is a contradiction—a ski instructor who's scared of heights, and a passionate woman who's afraid of intimacy.

But a lost child, an approaching blizzard and a legendary Scot force her to face her fears, and re-examine her dreams. Dreams which are hanging by a cobweb-thin thread...

Chapter 1
MONDAY 9TH JANUARY 2006

A SOLITARY TEAR faltered its way over a smear of freckles on Fiona Easton's cheek, landing on a pristine white pillow which smelled faintly of lavender.

Outside, a robin's bright song mocked her, heralding the new day as early morning sunlight crept around the edges of the blinds. On her uncluttered bedside table, the alarm clock glowed like a beacon, showing that there was still an hour before it would erupt like a klaxon. But there was no point in closing her eyes again, she wouldn't sleep. Not now.

With a sigh, Fiona reached out an arm to switch the alarm off. At that very moment, another hand inched around her ribs. Her breath caught. *Geoff.*

Fiona's eyes widened as the hand continued its investigation northwards. For a moment, she lost herself, enjoying the sensation of her husband's rough palm on her smooth skin. But then memory intruded, and the pain resurfaced. In one explosive movement, she leaped out of bed, crisp white bedcovers flying everywhere in her wake, and headed to the bathroom.

GEOFF EXTRICATED himself from the tangle of sheets and threw himself back onto the pillow, banging his fist against the mattress in frustration.

He lay there for a minute, then levered himself upright with a sigh, and pulled on some clothes.

Ten minutes later, he was wearing an incongruous frilly pinny to protect his ski patrol uniform, and had a pot bubbling on the stove and coffee brewing in the percolator. Satisfied that everything was nearly ready, he crossed the small chrome and white kitchen in two steps, and stood at the open door to the living room. "D'you want sultanas in your porridge?"

The lounge was as tidy as its owner, a medley of beige and Ikea. Multi-tasking as usual, breakfast news accompanied Fiona's exercise routine, the TV blaring in the corner as she stretched out on the floor and counted sit-ups under her breath.

"Ninety-six... ninety-seven..." Her rhythm didn't alter. "Yes, please," she shouted, then finished her set. "Ninety-nine... hundred." Routine complete, she sat up, shook her head briefly as if dizzy, then jumped up and headed toward him, tucking her dark hair behind her ear.

He caught her around the waist as she passed him, and kissed her neck. "Good workout?"

"Fine, thanks" Her arm went up and round him in a quick hug, before she broke free and made for the kettle. "Want some coffee?"

"I've already made some—here." He handed her a mug.

With a sigh of pleasure, she cupped the drink in both hands and looked at him over the top as she inhaled the rich aroma. "You're too good to me."

"I know how much you like your unhealthy habits," he said with a wink.

The corners of her lips curled upwards. "I just don't think it's fair to leave a man drinking on his own."

He laughed, then went back to stirring the oats. But the repetitive action let his mind return to the scene in the bedroom earlier. Hard as it was, he needed to speak to her about it. Just so he could be sure where her head was at. Taking a deep breath, he glanced across at her. "So, you're not ready yet." A statement, not a question.

She frowned. "Yes, I am."

"But—" He dropped the wooden spoon into the pot.

"I need to get back to work. To take my mind off... things."

Ah. He tried to stop his jaw from clenching. She was right, though, work was definitely a panacea. He'd been glad of the busy days in the ski patrol office. So perhaps a few days mixing with other people up the hill would be good for her too, and get things back to normal for them. He nodded slowly and turned back to the porridge.

Chapter 2

RED-BERRIED HOLLY BUSHES and yellow-flowered mahonia peeked over the fences of the stone houses on the main street of White Cairns village, adding colour to an otherwise grey day.

Jude snuggled her chin into a red woollen scarf, watching as a small group of navy-uniformed children filed on to the school bus, which grumbled like an ill-tempered troll and belched diesel fumes into the frosty morning air.

She was about to turn away when the last teenager turned from the step to shout to her. "Don't forget, Mum, I've got drama tonight."

"Of course, Lucy, see you at four thirty." Jude raised her hand in final greeting, then made her way into the nearby ski school shop to check for mail.

Unlocking the door, her nose wrinkled. The air smelled musty, and, as she flicked on the light, she vowed to find some time for a spring clean. *Maybe there'll be a storm and the hill will be closed and we won't be able to work,* she thought.

Then she laughed at herself. It had only been a few short weeks ago that she'd been looking at the purple and green hills in the distance and praying for some snow to help her save a dying business. A dying business that she'd been totally unqualified—and unconfident —to run.

And yet now here she was, somehow managing the motley band of ski and snowboard instructors, bringing in new customers, and even making a little money.

As if to reinforce the point, she ripped open a bank statement that had been lying on the doormat, and breathed a heavy sigh of relief at the positive—albeit small—figure in the balance column. As recently as the end of last year, that column had been printed in red, and they'd been staring bankruptcy in the face.

That thought gave her pause. *They.* She ought to try and phone him today. *Allan.* Her other half, Lucy's father, and their usual chief instructor and manager, who had gone to New Zealand at the beginning of the summer to earn money for the business... money which had failed to materialise.

Her shoulders sagged, remembering the mournful international ring tone, and the interminable waits she usually suffered when she tried to phone him—if the call even connected.

Later. She'd try again later. Snapping off the light, she

locked the door. *The time difference will be better then, anyway.* For now, she'd better get up the hill and make sure those numbers didn't turn red again.

MIKE COLE CLAMBERED onto the single-decker coach, grabbed the first pillar with one hand, and put his rucksack on the floor. Assorted items of skiwear adorned seat backs, empty crisp packets were strewn about the gangway, and there was a general air of subdued excitement throughout the vehicle—with the exception, perhaps, of the driver, who chewed on a matchstick and looked bored to the back teeth.

In the front seat, Mr Paton, the brusque, balding, forty-something head of P.E., looked up from typing something on his mobile phone. "Morning, Mike."

"Morning." Giving him a quick nod, Mike surveyed the passengers.

A few seats behind the teacher, a young boy was so entranced by a spider painstakingly making a web in the corner of the window that he was oblivious to the fact that his collar was tucked inside his fleece and that he was wearing mismatched gloves.

Further back, a group of teenage girls were giggling over a celebrity gossip magazine. And at the back of the bus, a fair-hared girl who looked to be about twelve going on twenty, queened it with her cronies. Mike narrowed his eyes, realising that she was making fun of another child, an unfortunate who was wearing last season's antiquated ski suit.

He raised his voice. "Good morning everyone." Most of the children looked up. "I'm glad to see you're all kitted out for skiing. Remember, fashion doesn't matter on the ski slopes—a designer label won't keep you warm and dry." He gave the 'it' girl a significant look. "Functionality is what's important. And the forecast for today isn't great, so make sure you remember your hat, gloves and goggles."

Giving the driver a thumbs-up, he sat down on the seat opposite Mr Paton as the bus crunched into gear and began to wind its way up the ski road. "Now, what groups do you have for me today, Mr Paton?" he asked, pulling a clipboard out of his backpack.

STUFFING a rustling pharmacy bag into one of the copious pockets of her ski school jacket, Zoë Agnew hurried toward the door of the shop, thanking her lucky stars that it opened early on weekdays. Otherwise, after the rather drunken night she'd had with Ollie, she might have been in *big* trouble.

Spoke too soon, Zoë, she thought, groaning in dismay as she spotted the ski area shuttle bus trundling down the street. If she didn't get to work on time, she wouldn't get paid, and she'd have to dip into her allowance to pay the rent. Which she definitely *didn't* want to do, since she'd come up here to demonstrate her independence. *But I might just catch it if I run!*

In a deft move that would've graced a top basketball player, she dodged around the only other customer in the shop, then raced for the door. Flinging it open, she bounded through, one eye on the approaching vehicle and the other on the bus stop she was headed for—and cannoned into something hard, ending up in an ungainly heap on the ground. "Oof!" All the air disappeared from her lungs.

Before she could draw breath and get to her feet, the bus sailed gaily past. Biting back a curse, she fought to extricate herself from what turned out to be an old-fashioned bicycle with a basket in front, laden with shopping bags which had burst, spilling groceries everywhere. *Just what I needed.* But maybe the next bus would get her up the hill in time for the start of lessons? *I could phone and say I'll be late.*

Her thoughts were interrupted by an insistent tapping on her arm. She turned to discover she was being glared at by a grey-haired old lady in a decades-old ski jacket, who was pinned on the ground by the fallen bike. "My messages." A bony finger pointed at the burst packets and the cans rolling ponderously toward the gutter.

Scrambling to her feet, Zoë did the best she could to round up all the escaping tins before they got squashed in traffic, then righted the bike and tried to help the cyclist to her feet. "I'm ever so sorry, I was trying to catch the bus and I just didn't see you."

This earned her a scowl, a grumble, and some prime side-eye that, if she'd been a character in a fairy tale, would probably have turned her to ice. It reminded Zoë of her grandmother, a formidable woman with an acid tongue who had been able to turn grown men into blabbering babies with just one stern look over the top of her horn-rimmed glasses.

With a squeal of brakes, the bus pulled in to the stop just down the street, and a surge of people crowded toward the door. *Maybe I can make it after all, if I can just get this old dear sorted*

Quickly, Zoë grabbed the pensioner by the elbow and yanked her to her feet. But, as soon as she was upright, the old woman's right ankle gave way and she almost fell over again, with a yelp that put Zoë's eardrums in severe danger of being pierced.

Watching in dismay as her only hope of getting to work in time closed its doors and pulled away in a puff of exhaust smoke, Zoë had no option except to help the injured cyclist to the step of the next-door charity shop, which was not yet open, and sit her down.

Like all the other instructors, Zoë had done First Aid training as part of her snowboard qualification. But she'd never expected to use it when kneeling on the pavement on the main street of The Cairns.

Palpating the woman's ankle to check it for pain nearly got her teeth kicked out. "Sore?" she asked.

The old lady gave her another milk curdling look and muttered something about the Pope.

I'll take that as a yes, then. Out loud, Zoë said, "I think you'll need to get to a doctor to get that ankle checked out. It might be sprained." *Or you might have chipped a bone,* she thought, but didn't dare say that out loud for fear of being turned into a frog. "Is there someone who could take you?"

"Yes." This was accompanied by bony finger pointing at Zoë's chest.

Me? Not likely. "Haven't you got any family here?"

"No."

Zoë sat back on her heels and surveyed the old woman. This was *not* how her day was supposed to pan out. She had better things to do than chase around after monosyllabic pensioners. But... she couldn't just leave the old biddy here. And she was already late for work. Perhaps if she could get an ambulance for the woman, she could get rid of her in time to catch the next bus.

"All right. Here's what we'll do. I'll go and find out how to get you to the doctor, okay?"

A minute later, she'd ascertained from the pharmacist that the health centre was within walking distance, if you didn't have a broken ankle, that an ambulance would probably take at least half an hour to arrive, and that, as far as she could remember, the old lady was Margaret Andrews, known locally as 'Mad Meg'.

With a sigh, Zoë returned outside, eyeing up the bicycle, torn shopping bags and bird-thin old lady. *Could I somehow wheel her round to the doctors?* Maybe the pharmacist would keep the groceries safe to save her carrying them. She went back inside to ask, emerged with a couple of fresh plastic bags and began to re-pack the shopping.

"Zoë, is it?"

She looked up in surprise. Striding towards her was Forbes Sinclair, the operations manager of the ski area, moustache bristling, cigar glowing and boots clomping as he bore down on them.

"Yes, Mr Sinclair." It felt like she was a naughty schoolgirl talking to her headmaster. She was surprised he even knew her name.

"What have we got here?"

"This old lady fell over—"

"Got knocked over," interrupted Meg, beady brown eyes glaring at Zoë.

"—got knocked over with her bike, and she's got a sore ankle. I'm working out how to get her to the health centre."

Forbes chewed on his cigar appraisingly. "Could take you in the old car if you want? Just need to pick up my paper first." He indicated the newspaper shop two doors away.

Chapter 3

SNOW SWIRLED IN THE AIR of The Cairns ski area's busy car park, shrouding the tops of the nearby mountains and turning the lower slopes into mere suggestions rather than beginner-friendly pistes.

Jude steered her grey estate car into the space beside a pine hut which proclaimed 'Lessons today!' in bold sans-serif, underneath a smaller sign saying 'White Cairns Ski School'. Craning her neck, she looked through the windscreen and peered up to where she knew the top of the Highlander run *should* be. But there was nothing to be seen. *Going to be a rough one today.*

When she got inside, she wasn't surprised to find all the instructors present. She smiled to herself. Having the slopes available to them every day was obviously turning them into fair weather skiers, and none of them had ventured out for a slide before lessons started.

In the background, a radio blared, and the red and blue uniforms of her team blurred in a flurry of activity. They were variously munching on junk-food breakfasts, exaggerating the previous night's exploits, fighting their feet into neat-fitting ski boots, reading the tabloids or stocking their pockets with the hats, goggles and other paraphernalia needed for a day in the mountains.

The shrill of the phone fought to be heard over the hubbub of noise, and Jude rushed to answer it. Her brows crept closer together as she listened to the female voice on the other end, then said a few words into the receiver and put the handset down.

At the whiteboard on the wall, Mike Cole, the New Zealander who had stepped in as chief instructor this season, was writing up class allocations. He turned as she approached, raising an eyebrow questioningly.

"Bad news," she said with a sigh. "That was Zoë, she's phoned in sick."

The tall, spare-looking Kiwi raised his eyebrows. "And guess who was still at The Rowan when I left last night? Looking very cosy with some guy with an eyebrow ring?"

Jude made a face and shook her head despairingly.

"She'll be right," said Mike, "I'll sort something out."

He rubbed Zoë's name off the board, then paused for a moment, rubbing his nose, before shouting over to the others. "Simon?"

Simon Jones, also known as Spock for his space-cadet tendencies, looked up from clipping on his ski boots.

"Could you take boarders today, instead of skiers?"

Simon nodded, and started undoing the ski boots, pulling snowboard boots out from under the bench and lacing them on instead.

A gust of wind rustled the pages of the newspapers on the table as the door opened and a pixie-faced, dark haired instructor entered.

"Fiona!" Jude hurried over and gave her a shoulder hug. "It's wonderful to see you!"

Her friend's thin shoulders under the uniform jacket were tense, and Jude quickly released the hug. She lowered her voice. "Are you really sure you're ready to come back to work?"

"I'm fine," Fiona replied. "Fighting fit." She made a face. "And it'll do me good to keep busy. There's only so many times you can clean an oven or rearrange your CDs. Being stuck at home was driving me crazy."

Jude looked at her sideways. "If you're sure. I know what you mean about keeping busy."

That earned her a sharp look from Fiona.

Flustered, she drew her friend further into the room and indicated the chief instructor. "You've met Mike. I'm sure he'll have classes for you today—Zoë's off sick."

CHUGGING up the main road in Forbes' Landrover, Zoë tried not to gag at the overwhelming smell of Havana that pervaded the vehicle. Crammed in the back along with the bicycle and shopping bags, her fingers itched for a cloth to wipe the mud from the door panels, and a bin to collect all the discarded papers and wrappers on the floor. When her room-mate, Debbie, had called her a 'neat freak' recently, she hadn't been wrong...

In the front, Forbes wasn't even trying to make conversation with Meg. Instead, he was holding forth in something of a monologue. "Been a difficult couple of weeks up the hill. Had to let one of the ski patrol go, so now we're a man down. And the forecasters have it that there's a blizzard coming through later today, which will keep the troops busy. And now the board are saying they want me to run the ski school race next month, so lots of prep to do for that..."

Zoë let his rhetoric wash over her, and instead, turned her mind back to last night. What she could remember of it.

Ollie had been good company at the Rowan, keeping her entertained with his stories of working as an instructor in Japan and Australia, and anecdotes about his colleagues in *Snowbound*, one of the other ski schools in the resort. She'd been intrigued by his eyebrow ring and the Celtic knot tattoo around his neck—which, she'd discovered later, wasn't the only ink he sported...

"That's us!" Forbes' loud voice interrupted her memories, as he stopped the four-wheel drive outside a single-storey building that looked like a bungalow on steroids. He hustled round to the other side to help Meg out of the

passenger seat and up the steps to the front door, leaving
Zoë to extricate herself from the back.

Then he proceeded to unload the bike and shopping.
"Got to love you and leave you, ladies," he said, touching
his forehead in an almost-salute. "Staff meeting up the
hill at," he checked his watch, "oh-nine thirty hours.
Ciao!"

Hands on hips, Zoë stared at the disappearing
landrover. With their transport gone, how was she going
to get the old lady home once they'd finished here?

A grumble from the entrance got her moving again.
One problem at a time, Zoë. Stowing the bicycle around the
corner and out of sight, she picked up the shopping bags,
pushed the door open with her hip and offered Meg an
elbow for support. *One problem at a time.*

MIKE SHOOK Fiona's hand enthusiastically. "Nice to see
you back, Fiona." He waved a hand at the board. "But I'm
having a 'mare. I was going to put you on adult ski school,
but I've been let down, and I'm really sorry, I need you to
do a school group today. D'you mind?"

"Don't worry, I'll be fine, honest," she answered,
trying to radiate confidence with her posture. But she
couldn't stop her eyes sliding sideways to glance at the
unfamiliar faces across the room.

"Have you met the others?" he asked. She was sure he
was trying to put her at ease. "You know Sandy, and Zoë's

off today," he pointed at the younger instructors in turn, "but here we've got Debbie, Marty, Ben, Callum and Simon."

Fiona replied to the chorus of greetings from the new members of staff with a small wave and a smile, before putting her daypack on the bench and starting to wrestle with her ski boots. They always felt two sizes too small in the morning, especially when they were cold.

Once the boots were on, she stood up to hang the bag on her peg, and realised that the other instructors were gossiping about ski patrol, which piqued her interest.

Sandy Potter, a rotund, balding, rather jaded fifty-something, known as Santa when not in earshot, was holding forth. "I mean, I don't know how Ski Patrol are going to manage without him. Doug practically ran the place, single-handed."

Fiona was surprised. Geoff hadn't mentioned anything about Doug.

"And nobody's sure if he jumped—or if he was pushed," Sandy continued.

Callum narrowed his eyes. "Probably the latter." He shook his head, making his messy ginger hair stick up at even more extreme angles. "But I thought they were short-handed? They'd better watch they haven't thrown out the baby with the bathwater."

A sudden silence filled the room, and everyone's eyes swivelled round to look at Fiona, faces registering a mixture of horror, curiosity and sadness.

She felt heat climbing up her neck, and quickly

dropped her head, clenching her teeth and studying her boots as if her life depended upon it. *Keep it together, Fiona, keep it together.* She'd made it this far, there's no way she was going to lose it now, not because of some silly man.

Chapter 4

OUTSIDE THE SKI SCHOOL hut, it was organised chaos. Groups of bundled-up children clutching skis and poles—with varying degrees of expertise and success—were shepherded by harassed-looking teachers to the meeting place. As groups were paired off with their instructors, they headed off in the direction of the ski slopes.

The instructors were easy to pick out by their bright uniforms and practised nonchalance. Using his height to advantage, Mike peered over the heads of the throng until he saw his target, who was standing outside the ski school hut, a distant stare isolating her from the hubbub.

But Callum reached her first. "Fiona!"

She looked sideways at the ginger-haired Scot.

"I'm really sorry about earlier. I was a real wally," he said.

"It's fine. You don't need to apologise."

"Aye I do—I need to learn to engage the brain before opening the cakehole." He raised an eyebrow. "It only took me three years at university to learn how to be this stupid!"

Fiona laughed, and Mike found himself grinning too as he interrupted them. "Fiona! Can I point you at your group?"

Callum disappeared with a shrugged wave, and Mike looked down at Fiona. "Are you really sure you're up for it, today?"

"I'm fine. You know what it's like," it was as if someone flicked a switch, "I'll just go into 'teaching mode'." She gave him a big smile. "See?"

He looked sideways at her, unconvinced. But he'd have to give her the benefit of the doubt. Maybe he'd get some time later to go up the hill and check on her. "No worries." He passed over the class list. "Ten of them today. Plus the teacher."

Her class were bunched restlessly beside Mr Paton, who seemed more interested in his mobile phone than in his charges or the day's activities.

Mike waved an arm, remembering what they'd discussed on the bus earlier. "Here's your group. Been skiing a couple of days now, so most of them are doing good snowplough turns and they're ready to move on." He motioned to the teacher. "And this is their teacher, Mr Paton. He'll be your helper today."

"Morning!" Fiona's smile encompassed the group. "My name's Fiona, I'm going to be your instructor today.

Are you all ready?" Judging by the bright faces of her class, her excitement seemed to be infectious. "Then let's go and do some skiing!" She picked up her skis, swung them onto her shoulder, and led them off towards the ski tow.

Maybe she'll be okay. Mike started to raise a hand in farewell, then let it drop to his side when he realised it wouldn't be seen by the departing group. *Hopefully.* With a glance at his clipboard, he went off to sort out the next item on his list.

AN HOUR LATER, Zoë was once more wrestling with the bike as old Meg disappeared round the corner in the comfort of a local taxi.

After the mind-numbingly boring wait for Meg to get seen, alleviated only by some out-of-date gossip magazines and some watery vending machine tea, Zoë had decided it would get her finished quicker with the pensioner if she paid for a taxi rather than waiting for the local ambulance, which was currently busy up the hill fetching some skier who'd fallen on ice.

But that left her to cycle, via a shortcut and some rather sketchy instructions, to the old lady's house on Railway Terrace. It was years since she'd ridden a bike, and whoever it was that said you never forget had been lying. It was just as well she'd managed to get the shopping bags into the taxi, even if he wouldn't also take the bicycle. She could never have managed to drape two bags of groceries from the handlebars and still stay upright.

One near miss at a pedestrian crossing, two blaring horns and three slipped gears later, with a judder of brakes, Zoë drew up outside a detached stone villa with a slate roof, outbuildings attached to the left-hand side, and a well-tended garden.

This was where the old lady lived? She'd have imagined a tumbledown shack. Or maybe a cave... She fought the smile that tried to blossom at that thought.

The taxi must only have arrived a minute or so earlier, as he passed her after turning at the other end of the cul-de-sac. Meantime, Meg was hobbling up the garden path on the crutches the clinic had given her, right ankle encased in plaster, groceries left forlornly at the gate.

Picking them up, Zoë wheeled both them and the bike up to the house. Her aim was to get the old lady and her things into the house, then get out of there as quickly as possible. Perhaps there'd be an afternoon class to be had up the hill. Or she could just go for a ride on her snowboard. With luck, she could still wring something useful from her day.

CALLUM SURVEYED HIS CLASS, a group of teenage girls. His lack of boy-band looks didn't seem to deter them—there was a lot of nudging and giggling going on. Obviously a ski instructor was a catch, no matter what he looked like.

He managed to internalise his eye roll. It was going to be a long day.

Hoisting his skis onto a shoulder, he beckoned them to follow him. "C'mon, gang, let's go hit the slopes," he paused for effect, "and hope they don't hit us back!"

With much hair-flicking and hip swinging, his group started to follow him. After only a few yards, one of them, sporting a black ski suit and womanly wiles well beyond her years, contrived to drop her skis. "Oh!" She said, looking pleadingly at him, a curtain of black hair falling over her matching eye-makeup. "Can you...?"

This time Callum couldn't hide the eye roll. "Seeing as it's you." He picked up her skis and loaded them onto his other shoulder, pretending he didn't notice the thumbs-up her friend gave her. Today was going to be an *exceedingly* long day.

DEBBIE AND MARTY watched the pantomime of Callum's class and the dropped skis while they waited to be given their groups. Marty shook his head, "How does he do it? I mean, he's not even good looking—his nose is all squidgy and that forehead goes on forever!"

"I dunno," Debbie shrugged, "maybe they think he's funny or something, women usually like that."

Callum was too short and ginger to be her type, but Marty... She studied him surreptitiously. From the side, she could see how long his eyelashes were, and the way his hair curled round his collar made her wonder what it would be like to run her fingers through it. But she'd never have a chance with someone like him, unless maybe she could impress him with her skiing. Perhaps he'd notice her then, if she could pull off some tricks or win a race or something. *Yeah.* Like that was ever going to happen.

"They must have a weird sense of humour, those girls. I mean..." Marty's theories on women were cut off by the arrival of Mike, brandishing class lists.

"Right guys, plenty of time for chatting later." He motioned for them to follow him. "Let me take you to your groups."

Chapter 5

ZOE'S PLANS WENT AWRY the minute she entered Meg's house. The old lady's abode looked like a bomb had hit it.

Or actually... no. Zoë examined the hallway calculatingly. There was just a lot of *stuff*. In piles. Everywhere. Stacks of magazines, mostly about skiing or gardening, a box overflowing with shoes and boots, a line of wellington boots in various states of disrepair, a heap of jackets, another jumble of ancient ski wear...

She picked her way through the disorder and followed Meg to the kitchen, where she stared, open mouthed, at the cluttered work surfaces and overflowing cupboards.

If she'd thought that the kitchen in their shared house was bad after Spock had done his turn at cooking dinner, she'd been living in cloud cuckoo land. The doctor's words, as she'd taken Zoë aside after discharging the old lady, swam back into her brain. '*...confused... off her meds... should improve in an hour or so once the pills I've given her kick in...*'

Meg obviously had some... issues. Which might explain her nickname in the village, why she hadn't done much in the way of chatting in the short time they'd been together, and why her house looked like this. A little of Zoë's irritation at her day being turned upside down dissipated. The old dear couldn't really help it. "Where would you like me to put the shopping? I'll unpack it for you if you'd like."

With a jerk of her chin Meg indicated a door in the far wall, which turned out to be an old-fashioned pantry. With white-painted shelves and lime washed stone walls, the larder definitely had a cooler air than the rest of the house. It was also relatively tidy and organised, which made a pleasant change, and made it easier for Zoë to unpack the groceries.

By the time she emerged back into the kitchen, Meg had put the kettle on and two earthenware mugs were sitting on the counter beside a china teapot.

Zoë stifled a sigh. So much for her afternoon up the hill.

Coire Beag was a wide, gentle slope, with good snow cover; ideal conditions for shaky intermediates. Part-way down, Fiona had arranged her class in a vertical line up the side of the piste, to minimise obstruction to other skiers. Under lowering skies, they watched as Fiona used her arms in sweeping movements to demonstrate a ski manoeuvre, then showed them how to do the exercise.

Mr Paton, at the bottom of the line, wasn't paying attention. Fiona could hear him muttering secretively into his mobile phone: "...in the three thirty... Yes... Okay. Thanks." She narrowed her eyes at him, and he snapped the phone shut, just as Amanda, a fair-haired girl who seemed to be the ringleader of the girls in the group, finished her turn.

"You're a star, clever girl!" Fiona called to her, and then addressed the group. "Right, you've all done so well, I think you're ready to go over to Ceann Mòr. Amanda, can you lead the class down to the bottom?"

Amanda seemed to grow a couple of inches taller as she set off, the rest of them following her like Hamelin's children after the Pied Piper.

Johnny, the youngest in the group, with mismatched gloves and oversized salopettes, was the last-but-one to go. As he pushed away, his red scarf fluttered to the ground.

Mr Paton, the final skier in the group, picked it up for him, and turned to Fiona, shaking his head. "Kids—who'd have 'em?"

His flippant comment was like a spear to Fiona's heart, and she had to take a moment to compose herself before hurrying off to catch up with the group.

GEOFF TAPPED a finger on his pen as he listened to Forbes Sinclair, the middle-aged operations manager of the chairlift company, who was giving their daily briefing. He'd been sitting beside the window in the wood-panelled ski patrol office at a desk containing their radio set and a stack of file trays, filling out paperwork—until their boss arrived and interrupted him.

"He went under something of a cloud, I'm afraid," Forbes was saying, warming his corduroy-clad legs at the gas heater blasting away in the corner, "and it's left us in a bit of a bind. A man down and all that."

Putting his biro back on the desk, Geoff took a quick glance round at the rest of the team, assessing their mood. "Don't worry, we'll manage until you get someone else," he said. "I guess we could do extra shifts, if the guys are up for it." Fiona wouldn't like it that he would be working longer hours, but there was no choice really.

"Good of you, good of you. That's a help," Forbes replied and then paused, giving Geoff a brief sideways look. "And of course we'll be looking for a new senior ski patroller to replace Doug. The advert will go up shortly."

Despite himself, Geoff felt his hopes raise. He wouldn't be the only candidate for the job, he was sure, but it would be great if he could get the vacant post. And maybe Fiona would be happier if he got a promotion. He balled his fists. He'd just have to work hard, and prove himself worthy. He could do it, surely he could?

OVER AT THE Ceann Mòr tow, Fiona was organising her class into the queue. One at a time, skiers and snowboarders straddled the plastic 'buttons' suspended from the ascending tow line at the bottom of short metal poles, and were dragged upwards until they reached the top, where they would release the button and slide away. But Ceann Mòr was a long tow, stretching so far up the hill that you couldn't see the top, and the poor visibility on that particular day meant that the riders disappeared into the mist after about a hundred yards.

At the bottom of the tow cable, a small hut housed the machinery and provided shelter for Davie, the liftie, a rough and ready bloke who looked like a roustabout, but had a fanatical love for Elvis Presley songs. Even on the worst days, the dulcet tones of The King would serenade the clients as they ascended the tow. And on an especially bad day, Davie would join him in a discordant duet.

"Right, guys, Mr Paton is going to go up first," Fiona told them, raising her voice to be heard over Elvis' version of *'It's Now or Never'*. "When you get to the top, I want you all to wait with him until I get there—I'll be going up last. Remember, if you fall off the tow, just ski back down to the bottom, and Davie here," she pointed over at Davie, who nodded back, "will let you skip the queue and get straight on." She smiled round at them. "But you're all such great skiers that I'm sure you'll get right to the top, first time. Won't you?"

Those of the children that were paying attention confirmed their agreement as Mr Paton got on the tow.

The pupils followed him, one by one, helped by Davie, who was humming under his breath. Fiona, thankful he wasn't actually singing, waved at him as she got on last. "See you later."

Chapter 6

CROSS THE MOUNTAIN on a different run, Callum was waiting with most of his class for the final two girls to come up the Sneachda Deàrrsach tow. He was frowning across the valley at the looming blue-grey clouds, not really paying attention to his group until his Spidey Sense alerted him that something was brewing.

Natalie—the vamp in the black ski suit—had obviously elected herself as spokesperson. "Callum?" she said. The missing two girls joined the bottom of the group as she continued, "We were wondering, what d'you *do* when you're not teaching skiing?"

He raised one eyebrow. He knew fine well what she was getting at. Should he tell her that his heart belonged elsewhere? Except... for lassies like that, it made things even more of a challenge, didn't it? *Probably best to say nothing then.*

"In the summer, I mean," she clarified.

Thinking on his feet, Callum struck a pose. "Can you no tell?"

They just looked at him, thick black eyeliner making them look like they'd not slept for a week.

He put his arms out and mimed losing his balance. "I'm a tightrope walker. At Blackpool Tower."

Natalie smirked, and muttered an aside to the other girls. "Guess where I'm going for my summer holiday?" That provoked a fit of giggling.

Callum smiled wryly to himself. If only they knew how often ski instructors got asked that question, and how seldom the replies were true.

"C'mon, we can't stand around here all day!" He beckoned for them to follow him, then quickly skied off, shouting over his shoulder, "Parallel turns, all the way to the bottom!"

MEG PUSHED a pile of newspapers to one side and motioned for Zoë to sit on the couch, then hopped to an armchair by the fireplace, which was the only clear space in the room. Zoë placed Meg's mug of tea beside her, and put her own on a pile of books by the arm rest of the settee.

The lounge had a lot in common with the hall: good furniture, overwhelmed by chaos and disorder. Zoë tried not to let her face show the distaste she felt as she took in her surroundings. But she must've failed in that, as Meg's eyes narrowed at her.

Before the old woman could say anything, Zoë jumped up to examine some photos on the mantlepiece more closely. "You were an instructor?" She asked, lifting one of the dusty wooden frames, which contained a photo showing a group of happy skiers wearing the same jackets and salopettes. It looked to have been taken at some point in the eighties, judging by the lurid fashions.

"Yes," Meg said. "For nearly forty years."

More than one word! Zoë tried to hide her surprise at the polysyllabic response, and did some mental arithmetic. "So—you must have started when the resort opened? Or very soon after."

"Yes."

"Can I ask, why did you stop?" Much to the chagrin of her parents, Zoë was enjoying her work as a snowboard instructor, and couldn't understand why anyone would give it up.

The old woman grimaced. "Retired. Got too old, they said." She muttered something under her breath, and then said, "Wanted the bright young things, I reckon. Face didn't fit."

There wasn't really an answer to that. A change of subject was called for. "I would guess you're not from around here. With your accent, I mean."

"No."

Fiddlesticks. The pensioner had clammed up again, just when Zoë had got her talking for the first time since they'd met. Maybe skiing was the answer to conversing with Meg.

"So how was it you learned to ski? Did you take lessons once you arrived up here?"

A shake of her head. "Switzerland. Davos."

Zoë blinked. Even these days, Switzerland was expensive, and Davos was one of the most exclusive resorts, favoured by royalty and the rich. She looked around the room again. Could Meg come from a rich family? It might explain how she could afford a larger house like this on a ski instructor's pension.

Putting the photo down, she perched on the couch and took a sip of her tea. The tannin immediately coated all her teeth and chased away any final shadows of last night's excesses. Then she took a closer look at the mug, and compared it with the one Meg was holding. "This is hand made?"

"Yes."

That accent was definitely English. Somewhere south, near London, if Zoë wasn't mistaken, with overtones of Oxford or some decent school.

"Made it myself." Suddenly the old woman jumped up and grabbed her crutches. "Come! I'll show you."

Mystified, Zoë followed Meg to the kitchen, where the retired instructor led them through another wooden door beside the pantry, emerging in what looked to be one of the outside buildings she'd seen from the garden.

Except it wasn't just any old building. It was a studio, a potter's studio, with a wall of windows to let in light, hundreds of shelves filled with lustrous earthenware, and a large wheel dominating the centre of the room. Zoë's jaw dropped.

Meg had already peg-legged across the floor and was sitting at the wheel. She motioned her companion over. "Come. Have a try."

As SHE WAS PULLED up the hill by the the Ceann Mòr tow, Fiona was multi-tasking—zipping the neck of her jacket to keep out the cold and adjusting her goggles—when she noticed one of the children sitting on the snow to the side of the tow track just ahead.

She shouted, cupping a hand round her mouth to help her voice carry through the wind. "Get up and ski to the bottom and get back on again. We'll wait for you at the top!"

As she drew level with the child, she realised that it was Amanda, and that she was crying. She sighed. There was always one.

With a grimace, she got off the tow, leaving the button seat bouncing along the track until the spring mechanism reeled it in, and slid down to where Amanda was sitting.

"What's wrong?" It was hard to tell under all the layers of clothing, plus hat and scarf. "Are you hurt?"

Amanda shook her head.

Fiona shuffled over and went to take her elbow to

help her up. "Right, let's get you going, and we'll go back down to the tow so we can join the others."

Aided by Fiona, Amanda got to her feet. Then she stuck out her bottom lip. "Don't want to."

"What? But they're waiting for us at the top. They'll be missing you."

Amanda folded her arms stubbornly. "Don't want to go."

Fiona frowned. Maybe if she could get her to the bottom she would make more sense. "Well, we can't stay here. How about following me down to the bottom of the tow? D'you think you can manage that?"

Amanda nodded, sulkily.

Well, that was easy! "Right, in behind me," Fiona told her. "Just snowplough, there's not enough room for anything else. Slowly."

They set off down the side of the tow track, heading for the tow station down below.

IN THE SKI PATROL OFFICE, the phone rang. Geoff's hand shot out automatically, and he picked it up. "Okay... Uh-huh..." He put down the papers he'd been reading and sat back in the chair. *Oh boy.* "Okay... Right, thanks for that, will do. 'Bye."

Putting the phone down, he turned to Forbes, who was pouring tea into a china cup. "Bad news, I'm afraid. That was the Met Office. There's a major storm coming in. So we'll need to close the ski centre and get everyone down to the car park." He saw Forbes's expression. "Sorry."

"Not your fault, man, blame the weather," Forbes said, putting his untouched drink on the desk. "Right-ho, I'd better go and tell the ticket office staff and get signs put on the car parks. Could you radio all the lift operators, get them to start herding people off the hill?"

"Okay, and once they're done," Geoff replied, "I'll radio the rest of the guys and we'll do a final sweep to make sure nobody's been missed."

Forbes raised a hand in salute as he left the hut. "Roger. Ciao."

BACK AT THE Ceann Mòr tow queue, Fiona was remonstrating with a stubborn Amanda, watched by Davie, who was standing just outside the lift hut, adjusting his scarf to try and disguise a grin.

"What d'you mean, you don't want to?"

"Want to stay here. I don't have to go with you."

"Well, I'm not allowed to leave you on your own. D'you not want to ski or something?"

There was no answer.

"Is it the lift, then?"

This got a flicker of response, and something clicked into place for Fiona. "Amanda, are you scared of heights?"

The girl nodded, reluctantly.

"And that's why you don't want to go up the big lift?"

Another nod.

"Can I tell you a secret?" Fiona said, conspiratorially, "I'm scared of heights too! Can you believe it, a ski instructor who's scared of heights? But, once I get used to the lifts, I'm fine."

Fiona gave a moment for her revelation to sink in, and looked up to the top of the hill. The weather was worsening.

"How about coming up on the same tow as me?" Fiona suggested. "Then you wouldn't have to be on your own—we can go together. And that'll let us catch up with the others—they must be wondering where we are."

The girl weighed her up, making her decision. "Okay."

"Brilliant! Right, let's get ourselves sorted out." Fiona directed Amanda over to the loading point.

Davie, who had been following the exchange, came over to help. "Now, girlie, you stand in front and put one ski either side of her right ski," he said to Amanda.

He checked with Fiona: "Your right leg's your strong one, lass?"

Fiona nodded in agreement as she arranged their position and waited apprehensively for the next button to arrive. Tandem rides up the lift with the instructor were usually reserved for young children, not eight stone divas. Fiona hoped her legs were strong enough.

The tow arrived, and Davie passed it to Fiona, who

slotted it between their legs. "That's it. There you go!" he said.

They were swept off up the hill to the sounds of a Vegas-cabaret version of *'The Devil in Disguise'*, which Fiona thought was ironically apt. She shouted back over her shoulder, "I like the music, Davie!" He had his walkie-talkie clamped to his ear and was looking worriedly after them.

But then Amanda shifted her weight, and Fiona quickly faced forwards again, tightening her stomach muscles and quadriceps to counteract Amanda's movement. *Concentrate,* she told herself. The girl's balance was all over the place. She rolled her eyes, glad Amanda couldn't see her expression. She'd be glad when this ride was over.

Chapter 7

MR PATON BANGED his arms against his sides in a futile attempt to generate some heat. It was turning into a whiteout, so bad that he could hardly see the top pylon of the tow, just a few yards away. The rest of the class were huddled together, snuggling into their scarves, or pulling hats over their ears. In the background, little Johnny jiggled up and down as if to warm himself. *Always was a bit of a loner, that one.*

A couple of shapes slid from the top of the lift and Amanda rejoined the group as Fiona skied over to the side of the run to speak to him.

"Thought you'd abandoned us," he greeted her.

"No, sorry, I just got held up trying to get one of the kids up the tow."

"Can you not do something about the weather? It's hellish up here. I can't feel my toes anymore."

"I wanted to speak to you about that. I can't teach properly in this—it's not safe; I won't be able to see everyone. I think it's best just to get them down the hill as quickly as we can."

"Sounds good to me."

"Right. Would you go back marker then, please, and pick up any stragglers?"

"Sure thing."

Fiona slid to the front of the group and gave them instructions. "Right, guys, we don't want to hang about here any longer—let's get out of this weather." She pointed down the run. "We'll ski down in a line, one behind the other, behind me, with Mr Paton at the end—like we did before. Everyone ready? Let's go."

The class snaked off behind Fiona and disappeared into the driving snow as Mr Paton pushed off, hoping his frozen feet would thaw enough to turn his skis when he needed them to. Wouldn't do to fall over at get lost in this weather.

HALFWAY DOWN THE RUN, Fiona slid to a halt and the children stopped, strung out behind her. It wasn't quite so wild here, but she still couldn't see the end of the line until they all stopped.

She started to count, but could tell just by looking that there weren't enough people there. She felt her chest start to constrict, and quickly side-stepped upwards so she could face the group. "Who's missing...?"

With that, Mr Paton and Amanda emerged from the whirling gloom and joined the class.

"She fell over, sorry," Mr Paton explained.

Fiona started her count again. "...eight, nine." She stopped. Muttered to herself. "No!" She turned to the group. "Someone's missing." The children started looking round at each other, trying to work out who wasn't there. Then Fiona figured it out. "Johnny! Did anyone see what happened to him? Mr Paton?"

Mr Paton shook his head. "He was there when we were waiting for you."

None of the youngsters had seen him, either. A few of them started to look worried as a particularly strong gust of wind whistled past and nearly blew over a couple of the smaller children.

Mr Paton was his usual helpful self. "We're never going to find him in this. We should get the rest of us down now, into the warm. We can send help for him when we get down."

"But we can't just leave him!" said Fiona. "Guys—wait here a minute with Mr Paton; I'll go and see if I can work out where Johnny's got to."

She stepped up the run, retracing their general direction. Adrenaline fuelled her movements, but she didn't get far before the class had disappeared from view.

The storm whirled around her, snow driving almost horizontally into her face. She could see nothing, could barely tell which way was up. Desperately, she looked from left to right, but still saw nothing.

She shouted. "Johnny!"

The wind threw her voice back in her face, its howling deafening any chance of hearing a reply, and mocking her paltry efforts to be heard. Where could he be? Her throat constricted, and she swallowed, aware that the empty feeling in her stomach was back again, the familiar feeling of loss threatening to engulf her once more. She closed her eyes and breathed out hard, once, twice, again. *Calm yourself! Stay strong and you'll find him.*

The children were tortoising into their collars to keep the wind out, but looked up expectantly as she returned to the group.

She shook her head. "I'll have to look for him later."

Mr Paton looked smug.

"Let me just phone to report what's happened," she added.

She dug her mobile phone out of an inside pocket, lifted her goggles to see the screen properly and blinked the snow away from her eyes. But what she saw made her shake her head in exasperation, and helped bring her focus back into the here-and-now.

"There's *never* any signal up here. So much for full coverage." She tucked the phone away again. "We'll just have to ski down and get Davie to radio it in."

She turned to the group. "Right, in behind me, like before. Mr Paton, you're back marker again." As she turned to ski off, she muttered under her breath, "And try not to lose anyone else, this time."

DAVIE PEERED ANXIOUSLY through the window of his hut, eyes straining to see through the driving snow. When Fiona's group finally appeared at the bottom of the run, he felt a wave of relief wash over him. She came hurrying over, obviously wanting to speak to him, so he pulled his hood up and went back outside. "There you are!"

"Davie, can you radio down to Ski Patrol for me? One of my kids disappeared somewhere on the top half of the run—he was with us at the top, but we'd lost him by half way. You can't see a thing up there."

"Nobody saw where he went?"

"No. The teacher was at the back, and he didn't see anything. Can you radio the patrol, and then help the teacher to get the kids to the bottom? I need to go and look for him." She made to get on the tow.

"Wait, you canna do that, lass, the hill's closed. Leave him to Ski Patrol. That's their job."

Fiona grabbed a button as it came past and got on. "I can't, Davie, I've got to go." Her voice cracked. "I've already lost two children, I can't lose another."

As she swooped off into the storm, Davie shook his head at her stubbornness, then frowned and pulled out his radio.

Chapter 8

FOR A NEAT FREAK, Zoë thought she was coping rather well with the stained towel draped over her snowboard trousers, and the muddy hands cupped around the clay on the potter's wheel. It had started as just an amorphous lump, but now, thanks to Meg's instruction, bore quite a close resemblance to a bowl. A fruit bowl, maybe.

"Good!" Meg handed her short length of wire with wooden handles at each end. "Now release the piece. Reduce the speed of the wheel, then place the wire on the surface at the far side, and draw it slowly towards you."

A minute later, Zoë was looking proudly at her first item of what Meg told her was called 'greenware'. She kicked herself for not trying pottery during art classes at school. But she'd enjoyed painting too much, and had never branched out. Sadly. "May I decorate it now?"

The old lady shook her head, and pointed at a shelf nearby. "Put it over there to dry. It'll get its first fire tomorrow. *Then* you can decorate it, before the final firing."

Tomorrow. It sounded like the old lady was expecting her to come back. Zoë looked at her watch, and was surprised to find that it was early afternoon. Where had the time gone?

She sighed. There was no chance of going snowboarding now, but, then again, the wind had picked up and it probably wouldn't be much fun up the hill anyway. *I'm better off here.* And throwing the pot had been fun.

After washing their hands at a butler sink in the corner, Meg produced some cheese and biscuits, and they proceeded to eat, perched on stools at a bench in the window and surrounded by Meg's colourful ceramics.

Zoë paused with a cracker half-way to her mouth, and indicated the plates, mugs and bowls that filled the shelves. "Is this how you make a living? Do you sell it?"

A curt nod. "Yes. Ski in the winter and make pottery in the summer. Tourists like it."

In Zoë's brain, a light bulb pinged on. *Could I do something like that?* It would beat living on a ski instructor's wage, which wasn't anything to write home about, and spending most of your savings travelling to New Zealand or Australia to work for their winter season when the Scottish snow had melted.

If she did things Meg's way, she could ski for the winter, and earn money in the summer to support herself. That would mean she'd never need her allowance, and her parents would have no control over what she did—or who she was seeing. A vision of Ollie with his sleepy brown eyes and his lazy smile briefly swam before her.

What her parents didn't seem to understand was that half of the reason she'd come up here was to get away from her mother's terrible matchmaking schemes. As far as Zoë was concerned, she was *far* too young to settle down. But her mother had different ideas, and thought that because *she* had been married by twenty, that Zoë should be too.

No way, Jose.

Zoë smiled. She had a plan now, thanks to this old dear, which meant that her day hadn't been wasted after all.

HAVING DELIVERED his class safely back to the school coach when the hill got closed, Callum waited by the door as they tried to maintain their cool and climb elegantly up the steps—an impossible task in clumpy ski boots.

Natalie contrived to be last on, and stopped beside him. She gave what he assumed was meant to be a seductive look and put a hand on his chest. "Thanks for today. It was great."

He looked down at her hand, then back up, raising an eyebrow. "Hope you learned something."

"Oh, I learned a lot," she dropped her hand but batted her eyelashes at him, then turned to climb up the steps. At the top, she turned back to him with what was obviously meant to sound like an inconsequential afterthought. "See you in the summer!"

His brow puckered.

"In Blackpool."

Callum raised his eyes heavenwards. "Yeah, see you." *But not if I see you first.* With a shake of his head, he shouldered his skis and headed back towards the ski school hut, his teenage fan club forgotten.

Just ahead, he noticed another blue and red uniform, and, recognising the curvy figure, hurried to catch up.

IN THE LONG, grey minutes of her ascent up the ski tow, buffeted by the howling wind and pelted by wet flakes of snow, it was impossible for Fiona not to imagine the worst. Try as she might, she couldn't help but visualise Johnny buried, broken—or just lost forever. *It would all be her fault. Again.*

But when she slid off the top of Ceann Mòr, she made a determined effort to force the negative images away. *It won't help me find him.* With a push of her poles, she skied over to the place where the class had been assembled earlier.

Blinking the snow out of her eyes, she examined the area round about. But nothing seemed obviously out of place. She frowned. Surely he had to be around here? With growing unease, she cupped her gloved hands around her mouth and shouted on him. But all she heard in reply was the howl of the wind. She tried again, louder this time, "Joooohnnnnyyy!"

As her voice died away, there was a momentary lull in the storm and a slight improvement in the visibility. Beyond some rocks at the side of the piste, she glimpsed something, and her eyes latched onto it. It was something red.

Taking off her skis, faltering in her haste, she used her ski poles to help her walk through the uneven snow outside of the run, where she discovered a patch of yellow snow. Nearby, a red scarf was caught between two rocks. She picked it up. He *had* to be nearby. So why didn't he answer?

The snow cleared again briefly, and her stomach cramped violently as she realised how near she was to the cornice. She shuffled back a step. It was bad enough being there in daylight, feeling like she was on the edge of the world and about to fall off. But in this storm, she couldn't see a thing through the driving snowflakes, which helped her vertigo a little, but didn't dispel her fear of heights.

She hunkered down carefully—extremely carefully— put her poles down, and tried to see over the edge without getting too close. "Johnny!"

A small voice answered indistinctly, "Help!"

Fiona almost fainted with relief. *I found him.* Gingerly,

she lay down on her front and wriggled forward towards the edge. With every inch that she gained she had to fight all her instincts to pull back, the proximity to the drop-off making her breathing ragged and causing her heart to hammer in her throat. But she *had* to get to him.

Johnny's voice came again as she crept forwards. "Help me!"

Then, with a sickening crump and the sensation of falling, the snow broke away from underneath her hand. Her stomach lurched as her chest lost its support and she started to slide, her hands grasping at thin air...

Chapter 9

I N THE CAR PARK, Callum had caught up with Debbie, whose uncomplicated prettiness and Rubenesque curves were a welcome antidote to the make-up and machinations of his teenage pupils.

"Debbie!"

Hearing her name, Debbie turned and blinked through the snow. He thought she perhaps seemed a tiny bit pleased to see him.

"How was your day?" he asked.

"Oh, not bad. Apart from the weather." She made a face. "How about you?"

"Oh, you know, the usual," he paused and raised an eyebrow, "fighting my way through blizzards, fending off sex-starved teenagers, saving the world!" He blew smoke off the top of an imaginary handgun. "All in a day's work, Miss Moneypenny."

He achieved his goal. She laughed. "What're you like?"

They walked on a few steps in companionable silence. Then Debbie turned to him mischievously. "What were you today, then?"

He stopped and put his skis down, striking the pose. "Tightrope walker." He wobbled convincingly, lost his balance and teetered on one foot. "At Blackpool Tower."

They both laughed, and Debbie shook her head at his audacity. "You should be an actor, not a ski instructor!"

He grinned. "I'll make that tomorrow's summer job." He held out an imaginary skull. "Alas, poor Yorick! I knew him well." He shouldered his skis again and raised an eyebrow at her. "Actually, that's a common misquote, the real speech is much longer."

Debbie raised her eyebrows in surprise.

"But it's too cold for Shakespeare," he continued, "let's get back."

Just then, a particularly strong gust hit them and Debbie stopped to pull the hood of her jacket up over her hat. "Did you hear, by the way?"

"Yeah, I know," he gave her a James Bond look. "I've been voted 'Most Eligible Ski Instructor in Scotland'."

She chuckled. "No, silly, it's serious. One of the lifties told me that an instructor's gone missing."

That pulled him up short. "Is it one of us?"

"He didn't know."

"Or didn't say." He started walking again. "I'll bet it's

Spock. That guy lives on another planet. It's gotta be him."

FIONA PANTED, her breathing shallow and fast as she blinked rapidly to clear her mind and get her focus back. How could she help Johnny if she let herself dissolve into a puddle of fear?

But she'd been lucky. The cornice had broken away from under her shoulder, revealing the edge of the cliff and nearly plummeting her over the edge. Somehow, she'd dug her boots in and managed to claw herself back into a safe position. Closing her eyes, she made a determined effort to slow her heart rate. *Don't lose it, not now, not now he's so close.*

Inching forward, even more carefully this time, she craned her neck until she could peer over the edge. *Thank goodness!* There was Johnny, stuck on a ledge down below.

But as she eyed the distance to the lost child, the impossibility of her task clogged her brain. How could she help him? The danger of that cliff edge was making it hard to think of anything else.

Gritting her teeth, she dragged her mind back from visions of falling. She needed to concentrate, focus, and fix her attention on finding some way to help him.

Preferably some way that didn't involve her getting any closer to the edge.

IN THE SKI SCHOOL HUT, Mike was updating the white-board, ticking returned instructors off a list, while Jude was changing bookings on the computer. Wind whistled round the walls of the hut, making the roof timbers creak and rattling the windows.

Over in the corner, Sandy, Ben, Marty and Spock steamed quietly as they removed damp uniforms and too-tight ski boots. In minutes they would start heading down the hill, back to the safety of the village.

"Make sure that nobody gets left behind," he started to say, when a particularly ferocious gust of wind crashed the door open and Callum and Debbie were blown over the threshold.

Callum was barely recognisable as he started peeling off the hat, goggles and scarf that covered every exposed piece of skin. He looked over to the benches, and spotted the disrobing earlier arrivals. He turned to Debbie, "It wasn't Spock, then." A bit louder, he asked the group, "Did you hear the news from Ski Patrol?"

Mike paused with the drywipe pen in his hand, "Yeah, they're closing the hill. D'you get your classes down okay?"

Debbie nodded, but Callum continued his story. "Aye, but no, I mean, did you no hear that one of the instructors is missing?"

"Oh no!" Jude looked shocked, "Is it one of ours?"

"I dunno, sorry."

Mike checked his list on the board. "Fiona's the only one not back yet." As he turned back to the group, he caught Jude's expression, and quickly pulled his jacket off a coat hook. "I'd better go see if I can find out."

"Thanks, Mike." Jude looked relieved. "Be careful out there."

Mike's arm stopped half-way down his jacket sleeve, taken aback by her use of that expression. She kept saying these things. It was spooky.

JOHNNY LOOKED up to see Fiona dangling his red scarf over the edge. How had she got that? He put a hand to his neck. How had he not realised it was missing? But it was good she'd found it. His mum would be annoyed if he'd lost it.

"Can you reach it?" she shouted.

He stood on tiptoe and stretched as far as he could. "It's too short, Miss, sorry."

"Are you sure you can't catch it?"

Screwing his face up with effort, he jumped as high as he could in the clumpy ski boots and grabbed for the scarf. But he missed it, and nearly overbalanced when he landed, brushing some snow off the cliff face with his arm as he recovered.

"Careful!" Fiona warned him.

"I'm okay." But the dislodged snow let him see the cliff face better. "There's a couple of hand holds here. Maybe I could climb up." He strained up towards them, but they were just out of his reach. "I'm sorry, Miss, I'm not tall enough." He stamped his feet. "And I'm getting really cold."

Above him, Fiona's face took on a look like his mother's did when she was going to get a big spider out of the bath. She scrunched up her eyes and took a big breath, then she shimmied round, positioning herself so her feet started to angle over the edge. Next, one leg started to inch over the precipice, hanging into nothingness. Johnny's heart was in his mouth.

She crept a bit further.

Then, with a soft crump and a cry of alarm, the snow gave way beneath her, and she fell over the edge in a flurry of snow.

Chapter 10

"KEEP, SELL, CHARITY or bin?" Zoë asked, holding up the final ski jacket. Then she twisted it around and poked a finger through a large hole in the arm, and pulled at the frayed cuff. "Bin, I think?"

"It could be mended." The old woman sounded petulant. Sat on an antique piece of furniture that Zoë was sure was actually a commode chair, she had her ankle propped on a pile of books and was waving her crutch like a baton.

"Well, yes it could. But even if it was, you wouldn't wear it, would you? It would hardly be waterproof any more. And," she motioned at the 'keep' pile, which, despite Zoë's ruthless efficiency, was considerable, "it's not like you don't have plenty of other jackets."

Meg sighed. "If you insist." She'd come out of her shell, somewhat, perhaps thanks to the doctor's medication, but more likely thanks to a morning spent teaching Zoë how to make a bowl, and an afternoon of decluttering, which Zoë had suggested she could help with in return for the pottery lessons.

"We can make a start on the lounge tomorrow," Zoë said. "It should be easier, now that the hall is clearer and we've got into a rhythm. I'll come round after work."

That earned her a grunt.

"But I'd better get going now." She picked up one of the plastic bin bags they'd been using to sort the hodgepodge of stuff. "I'll take this to the charity shop on my way to the bus."

"Want some more tea before you go?"

Zoë shook her head. "Sorry, no. It's starting to snow, so I'd better get back home before we get snowed in. But I'll see you tomorrow."

As MIKE STRODE across the car park, still pulling on his hat and gloves, he spotted Davie, Mr Paton and the rest of Fiona's class emerging through the blizzard. He raised an arm.

Davie peeled off from the group, his teeth chattering with the cold. "Fiona's still up the hill. I'm away off to ski patrol to check they're looking for her."

Mike grimaced. *I shouldn't have given her a school group. I should've known it would be trouble.* "We heard someone was missing. I'll get the full story from the teacher, and then we'll see what we can do."

"Okay."

"And get yourself inside. You don't want to be catching frostbite."

With a grunt, Davie disappeared off through the snow, and Mike hurried to catch up with the group. He needed to find out what had happened, and work out how he could fix things.

FIONA SAT AWKWARDLY in a heap of snow on the ledge, breathing heavily and rubbing her elbow. Somehow, she seemed to be in one piece. And somehow the wind seemed less ferocious here, as if they were in the lee of the hill. But it was still snowing heavily, and, if she wasn't mistaken, the light was starting to go. *Great.* Why had she thought this was a good idea? Oh yes, to get to Johnny, maybe help him climb up.

Shaking some loose snow off his jacket, Johnny crawled over to her. "Miss?" He looked concerned. "Fiona, are you okay?"

"Yes. I think so." She closed her eyes. "Just a bit woozy. I'll be alright in a minute." She tried to control her racing heart, and eventually her head cleared a little.

Once she'd recovered somewhat, she manoeuvred herself onto her knees and crawled carefully—ever so carefully—back towards the cliff face, away from the edge. It felt a little safer there.

Then Johnny give a shiver. His clothes weren't made for this weather, and were damp. His teeth began to chatter.

Realising that she was still clutching the red scarf, Fiona wrapped it around his neck and tucked the ends into his collar. Putting an arm round him, she cuddled him to her, not sure which of them it brought the most comfort. It was probably a total contravention of child protection regulations, but in a situation like this, she reckoned all the rules went out the window. *Or perhaps over the cliff.* She smiled briefly, then rolled her eyes at herself. How could she think this was something to laugh about?

Looking around her, she reached a decision. "Johnny, can you stay right back, for now? I'm going to check how solid this ledge is."

"Yes, Miss."

This time, she sat with her bottom near the back of the ledge and used her ski boots to kick at the snow near the edge and check there was solid rock underneath, cautiously at first, then a little harder.

When she was satisfied that it was safe, she scrambled carefully to her feet.

Johnny watched all this with interest. "It's a shame we couldn't just phone for a helicopter to come and get us, like James Bond or something."

Idiot! She allowed herself a hint of optimism as she dug her mobile phone out and examined the screen.

No signal.

She waved it around in the air, then checked again.

Still no signal. Why had she allowed herself to hope?

Hunkering down and hugging Johnny again, she buried her face in his hair, fighting off tears. What were they to do? Snowstorm all around, cliffs below, unreachable cornice above. It wasn't the best situation she'd ever been in, to say the least.

Chapter 11

ENTERING THE SKI PATROL office, Davie found Geoff directing operations as he and the other three ski patrollers stuffed rescue equipment into rucksacks.

"I'm really sorry, mate, I tried to stop her, but she wasn't having none of it, she insisted on going up on the tow. You know what women are like."

Geoff looked up from strapping his rucksack closed, the colour draining from his face. "It's Fiona? Fiona's the one that's gone after the boy?"

"Yeah. Didn't you know?" Davie clamped a hand to his mouth. "You didn't know! I'm sorry, mate, I thought I'd said. Sorry. Sorry."

"No, all we made out from your message was that an instructor had gone after a missing boy." Geoff shook his head. "Why would she do that?" He swung the rucksack over his shoulder, then seemed to answer his own question. "She's not been right, ever since..." he tailed off.

Davie pulled his mouth into a line. "Sorry." He never knew what to say in awkward situations like this. That was why he was happy to work on his own in the hut, listening to Elvis, enjoying the sun—when it shone—and passing the time of day with the skiers and boarders who used his tow. He could never be a ski patroller, their job was much too hard.

Pulling on his gloves, Geoff turned to the other patrollers. "C'mon boys, no time to lose!" In a flurry of activity, the four of them strode out the door, leaving Davie alone in the suddenly silent room.

SITTING beside Fiona at the back of the ledge, Johnny had his knees hunched up against the cold, and was playing with the tassels at the end of his red scarf, swinging them from side to side like a spider casting a web. He looked round at his instructor.

"Miss, we can't give up. We have to keep trying. Like Robert the Bruce."

She stopped fiddling with the velcro on her jacket cuffs. "How did you get here, anyway? What happened? We didn't see you leave the group."

"I needed the loo, so I went to go quickly behind a rock, before you went down the run. But when I tried to go back to the group, I fell through the snow and ended up down here. I was getting really frightened on my own."

Then he remembered something. "I don't know what happened to my skis, Miss. They must've got lost when I fell. Will I get into trouble?"

She looked up at the top, then back at Johnny with a lopsided smile. "I think that's the least of our worries."

"Are we stuck, Miss?" He felt a tickle inside. Was that spiders in his tummy? How did they get there? Or maybe it was just 'nerves' like Mummy used to say.

Fiona hadn't replied to him, she was just staring out at the snow with this sad look on her face.

"Miss, we'll make it eventually, we have to, even if we have to wait till the storm passes. We can't give up. Robert the Bruce didn't give up, and he went on to lead the Scottish army." He touched her arm. "If I was a bit bigger and stronger, I'd lift you up so you could escape and get help. I'm sorry I'm not strong, I'm not very good at P.E."

Fiona stared at him like he'd said something amazing. "Why didn't I think of that?" She scrambled upright, pulling him up with her, then eyed the distance between the ledge they stood on and the cliff edge above. "Johnny, d'you think if I lifted you up onto my shoulders, you could climb over the edge? Are you brave enough?"

He looked up at the edge, then nodded. "Yes." He could be brave. Like Robert the Bruce.

A big smile lit up her face. "Right, let's give it a try!"

ASSUMING from Davie's account that Fiona would be on the Ceann Mòr, Geoff and the other patrollers were casting around at the top of the run, struggling to see through their goggles in almost zero-visibility and trying to work out where Fiona and her pupil could have gone.

The cold hand of panic squeezed more and more tightly around Geoff's heart as he prodded the snow with a long pole. Where *was* she? And the boy. Surely *one* of them should be visible? Yes, it had been snowing hard. But he doubted there'd been enough for them to be buried. So why couldn't they see them?

Suddenly he hit on something hard, just under the surface. His breath came in ragged gasps as he squatted down and unearthed a pair of skis, half-buried in the snow. Hastily, he brushed accumulated snow off the tips.

'FIONA' was written in thick marker pen across the top of each turquoise ski.

With a surge of hope, he cupped his hands round his mouth and shouted to the others. "I found her skis! So she can't be far away." He motioned for them to fan out. "See if we can find footprints." Then a particularly strong gust of wind almost knocked him over, and buried the skis again. His spirits plummeted. How would they ever find *anything* in this weather?

WITH A WHOOP, Johnny scrambled over the edge. Fiona breathed a sigh of relief. *I did it. I saved him.*

As he dragged himself to safety, he kicked some more loose snow, which dumped down on Fiona, causing her to splutter. But it also exposed a potential foothold on the cliff above her ledge.

Johnny peeked over at her, unmindful of the danger. "See! I told you we'd make it if we didn't give up." Then he seemed to realise the distance that still lay between them. "How are you going to get up, Miss?" He paused, "Do you want me to go and get help?"

"No! It's not safe in this weather." She eyed the distance from the foothold to the top. "Anyway, I think I might be able to climb up, there's a step here. Can you keep back from the edge?"

She motioned him to move back as she explored the foothold with her fingers. Would she trust her slippery plastic boots to grip the rock face? The ledge seemed quite deep, so it might work.

But she felt weakness creeping over her, and a knot forming in her stomach at the thought of the drop below her. *Focus!* she told herself, then breathed out and tried to clear her mind of negative thoughts. She had to stay strong. *Remember Robert the Bruce.*

Searching around at the full extent of her reach, her right hand grasped a handhold, then she put her left boot onto the small ledge, and took a deep, steadying breath in preparation. *It's now or never,* she thought, as Davie's favourite song popped into her brain.

Then she swung herself up, but as she did so, she felt her energy disappearing, and the sensation of falling overtook her as her vision shrank and the world went black.

Chapter 12

THE SKI SCHOOL DOOR swung open in a flurry of snow, and Jude looked up hopefully. But it was Mike, not Fiona. "Is there any news?"

"Haven't heard anything about Fiona, sorry—but Ski Patrol are on the case." Mike took off his hat and goggles and brushed the loose snow from his shoulders. "I've checked, and all the kids are safely on the school bus, apart from the one that's missing, that is."

The school bus! Jude put her hand to her mouth. *Lucy.* "How could I have forgotten! I'd forget my own head if it wasn't..." She stopped herself, and looked pleadingly at Mike. "Mike, you couldn't do me a huge favour, could you?"

He came over to the desk. "Yeah, sure, what can I do you for?"

"I should have collected Lucy from school, after

drama practice," she looked at her watch, "five minutes ago. But I can't bear to leave here just now, not with what's happening to Fiona. Could you possibly take my car and go down and get her for me?"

JOHNNY'S EYES turned into saucers as Fiona collapsed backwards onto the ledge, and he felt like spiders were running crazy spirals around his tummy. "Miss?" he shouted.

There was no response, so he shouted again. But she remained there, as still as his action hero model was before he took it out of its box to play with it.

As time ticked by and she didn't move or say anything he felt the spiders growing into huge tarantulas, trying to swarm up his throat and take his words away. Then a gust of wind buffeted him, and he tucked his chin into his red scarf. He was glad she'd found it for him. He liked playing with its tassels.

But that reminded him. Would Robert the Bruce have given up? *No.* That was what he liked about the Scottish king. He was a hero, and Johnny wanted to be a hero too. So he tried again, louder this time, his voice cracking with the effort. "Fiona!"

There was still no answer, even though he'd shouted as loud as he possibly could. His shoulders slumped. She'd been so brave, trying to help him, and now she was stuck down there and he didn't know what to do. But she'd told him he had to stay here—and anyway, he didn't want to leave her.

Tears began to roll down his cheeks, and he wrapped his arms around his middle, trying to stop the tarantulas climbing up and taking his voice away. He gulped them down, feeling very alone. But it was a busy ski resort— maybe someone else would come by? There had been a lot of skiers on the lift earlier. He should let them know he was here. "Help!" he shouted. But his voice wobbled and was barely louder than a whisper. He took a deep breath and tried again.

IF ONLY SHE'D asked him something else. Anything else.

"I... I can't." Mike shook his head, upset that he wasn't able to help her. "I'm sorry, Jude, I just..."

Jude interrupted him, "The car's insured, it's alright."

He looked across at her. "It's not that." He couldn't bring himself to tell her the full story. "I don't drive. Sorry."

Jude deflated. "Oh. I never thought of that." She bit her lip and looked up at the ceiling, obviously trying to think of a solution.

"I'm sorry," he said again. Without thinking, he put out a hand to touch her shoulder, then caught himself, and dropped it. Fortunately, she hadn't noticed.

Clicking her fingers, she roused into action. "I'll get

Sandy to collect her. He won't mind." She picked up the phone and punched in a number.

Mike moved away to take off his jacket, glad that she couldn't see his face. He hated having to lie to her. But he just couldn't tell her the truth. Not now.

THE RELENTLESS WIND hit Geoff like a physical assault as he and his colleagues hunted fruitlessly through the blizzard at the top of Ceann Mòr. It was so frustrating—the driving snow blurred the distinction between ground and sky and made it almost impossible to see tracks or make out the shape of a lost skier.

And progress was annoyingly slow, because they had to keep almost within touching distance to avoid losing each other. *We'll never find her at this rate. Or when we do it'll be...* Geoff paused in his negative thoughts, tilting his head and closing his eyes to help him focus. Had he heard something? Maybe the tiniest, faintest sound carried on the wind, perhaps a voice shouting for help? Urgently, he motioned for the others to stop.

The noise came again. Not recognisably a voice, but a different pitch to the interminable basso profondo of the storm. Could it be them? Fiona or the boy?

With renewed energy, he pointed the direction and they rushed off towards the cornice.

Chapter 13

BLACK WRAITHS EMERGED out of the whirling snow, and at first Johnny thought he had been found by gigantic yetis who'd come to devour him. He cowered closer to the ground, and tried not to move or breathe. But the snowflakes were sticking to his eyelashes, and, as he blinked them away, he noticed that the snow monsters were wearing uniforms and goggles. So they were people, not yetis!

Feeling like his heart would burst, he called out to them, "I didn't do anything, she just fell over and I can't get her to answer!"

One of the black-clad men came over to him and wrapped him in a thin, silvery blanket. "Don't worry, wee man, we'll look after you now."

Another asked him, more urgently, "Where is she? Where's Fiona?"

Johnny's felt his chin tremble, and he swallowed hard, pointing at the cornice. "She's still down there. She was alright till a few minutes ago, Sir, then she just collapsed when she tried to climb up. I couldn't get her to answer, Sir, I'm sorry, I tried really hard."

The angry man whirled round and headed for the cliff edge, disappearing in a flurry of snow. Maybe he really *was* a yeti, just one who could speak English? Johnny would ask his science teacher when he got back to school. *If* he got back to school. He looked up at the man towering over him. Did yetis wear goggles?

"I'm sure you did everything you could, son, you've been really brave." The yeti-man who was looking after him squeezed him round the shoulders and smiled at him. "We'll get you down the hill soon."

"And back to school?"

"Aye, back to school, once we've checked you over to make sure you're not injured. You'll be back with your pals soon."

Yetis, even English-speaking, goggle-wearing ones wouldn't be this nice, would they? He must be a man. "Are you a man?"

White teeth appeared through his beard and he chuckled. "Aye, son, my name's Rab, I'm one of the ski patrollers here at The Cairns. And you must be Johnny. Your teachers were worried about you."

"Were they?" Johnny's heart glowed. He sometimes thought the teachers didn't even notice him. But they were *worried* about him? He glanced over at the cliff edge, where the rest of the patrollers were busy with some equipment. Fiona had been worried about him too, and he liked her. "Will she be okay?" he whispered.

"I hope so, son. They're just getting organised to go down to her. Then we'll find out."

SAFELY BACK ON the Beechfields school bus, Amanda was surrounded by an admiring audience, hanging onto her every word as she described her skiing exploits. "...and then she told me how she's scared of heights, and hates going up the tows, and would I go with her to stop her being scared?" She flicked her hair back off her shoulder. "So I had to go up the tow with her 'cos she wasn't brave enough on her own. Would you believe it? And she's got the cheek to call herself a ski instructor!"

FIGHTING DOWN PANIC, Geoff rushed to the edge of the cliff and slammed to his knees in the snow. Then he took a deep breath, reminding himself that he needed a cool head and all his professionalism if he was going to help Fiona. *Treat it like any other rescue*, he told himself. Gritting his teeth, he leaned over the edge.

There was a moment of relief as he spotted her lying

only a short distance below him on a snowy ledge. But then the fear came slamming back, because she wasn't moving and he couldn't tell if she was breathing or not. Hunkering back, he blinked rapidly to clear his vision, fighting back the tears.

Beside him, two colleagues were already in the process of setting up an abseil belay. "Get the stretcher, Geoff," one of them shouted across to him, "we'll lower you down."

His pulse racing, he stumbled over to their pile of equipment and set about fixing a rope sling around his body and strapping the stretcher to his back, fumbling as the wet snow made the cords slippery.

In the background Geoff could hear Rab, who was looking after Johnny, speaking into his radio, cupping a hand in an attempt to be heard over the howling wind as he organised for an ambulance to meet them at the base station. *Good. At least he's thinking ahead.*

Seconds later, they were ready. Giving a brief thumbs-up, Geoff clipped himself on to the belay rope below the anchor-man, and walked backwards to the edge, releasing the rope through his hands as he went.

Getting over the edge was usually the hardest part of an abseil, but the snow was actually a help here, creating some natural steps, allowing him to get himself into the position where he could 'walk' backwards down the cliff.

He went as quickly as he dared, using his lower hand on the rope to control his speed and turning his upper body slightly sideways so he could check the face for loose rocks as he went. Through the snow, he could see Fiona's white face below him, and it seemed to take forever to reach the ledge where she was. He prayed she'd be okay.

Chapter 14

DARKNESS WAS FAST approaching and only a few lights still glowed in the recesses of the monolithic school building behind her as Lucy stood outside the gates, stamping her feet and blowing on cupped hands in a futile attempt to get warm.

Snow flew almost parallel with the road, speckling her head and shoulders as she peered hopefully at every passing vehicle. Where *was* her mother? And why did she have to be late, today of all days, when the weather was foul and the air was cold and the clouds were so grey and so low that it was already dark. *I hate the dark.*

Then an unfamiliar car drew up at the pavement, and Lucy stepped back in alarm. *Stranger danger!* She checked the street around her to see if there was anyone she could shout on for help. But it was empty, and she was just debating whether she could run faster than a car when the window wound down and she recognised the man inside. *Santa.* Or Sandy, as her mother insisted she called him. She much preferred Santa, like the others called him behind his back. It made her feel like she was a part of the instructor group, and cool like Marty or Zoë.

"Lucy!" Sandy shouted, his white beard moving up and down as he spoke. She'd never noticed that before. It was a bit like the way those puppets talked on that programme—what was it called? The old man's voice interrupted her deliberations. "Your mother asked me to come and get you. She's got held up, up the hill."

"You mean, she's forgotten me again?"

"No, she had to stay up there. One of the instructors has gone missing. The snowstorm, you know?"

Lucy narrowed her eyes. That was a good story. Almost 'the dog ate my homework' worthy. But it wasn't the first time her mother had been late, and there was always some extremely urgent reason. One day she'd write a story about it. Or a play. 'The Unbelievable Excuses of a Highland Housewife'. Or '101 Reasons to Forget Your Daughter'. She could see it now. She would have a starring role, of course, and the critics would love it. Maybe it could open at The Palladium?

"There's a child missing too. One of the pupils. Ski Patrol are out looking for them. However I doubt they'll get found in this." He shook his head. "But your mother was worried about you, so she sent me," Sandy continued. "Come on, get in, let's get you home out of this cold. You'll catch your death."

He had a point there. Reluctantly, Lucy swung over

and got into the car, closing the door a little more loudly than necessary. No doubt she'd get the full story when her mother got home. But, in the meantime, she had a soliloquy to compose.

Quickly, Geoff unclipped the stretcher and propped it against the rock face, his heart hammering and his fingers like fat sausages as he hurried to release enough rope to let him safely reach Fiona. Holding his breath, he leaned over to check if she was still alive.

His relief as he realised that she *was* breathing washed over him like a surfer's wave breaking on a sand-bar. But why was she unconscious? "Fiona! Fiona! Can you hear me? Wake up. C'mon, wake up." There was no response. He frowned, then quickly checked her head and body for breaks, bumps or wounds. But he found nothing that would explain her condition.

While he ran through possible diagnoses in his head, he pulled a neck brace from his pack, sliding it carefully underneath her hair and fixing it on. It was standard procedure, but it would also protect her, just in case there was something he'd missed.

But what could it be? She was unconscious but with no obvious injury to cause it, and she wasn't on drugs, or allergic to anything that he knew of.

It *must* be a head injury, he decided, just one he couldn't feel. With luck it wouldn't too bad, and they could stabilise her once they'd got her down the hill and were out of the storm. He clenched his fists, and went to get the stretcher. Hopefully she'd be okay. She didn't deserve this, not after everything.

JUDE RUBBED at the fog on the window of the ski school, trying to distinguish what was happening across the car park. Through the swirling snow and gusting wind she caught glimpses of an ambulance waiting outside the Ski Patrol hut, and various people going in an out, but no obvious sign that they'd found Fiona or the missing schoolboy.

All of the instructors apart from Mike had gone home, and he was sitting at the counter, sorting out class allocations for the next day. She suspected he was nearly as worried as she was, as he would look up any time he heard a noise outside. *He probably blames himself for giving Fiona that school group.*

Suddenly, grey shadows materialised through the driving snow, sliding down the final short slope to the car park. "That's them back!" she called to Mike as she rushed to collect her jacket from the pegs by the door.

Geoff was in the lead of the rescue group, holding the long handles of the sledge with its precious burden behind him, his skis in a wide snowplough to control the speed and smooth the ride. One of the other patrollers carried a child on his back, *so it must be Fiona on the stretcher.* Jude's anxiety ratcheted up a notch.

Zipping up her jacket, she strode across to them, Mike following closely behind. Blinking snow from her lashes, she saw Rab set Johnny down onto the ground, and the paramedics in vivid reflective jackets busying themselves at the sledge.

She put a hand on Geoff's arm. "Geoff..." He didn't take his eyes from the action at the stretcher. "What happened?" she asked.

"We don't know, we found her unconscious." He paused, glancing briefly in Jude's direction, his face a mask of worry. "The wee boy's okay, though—a bit cold and shaken, but he should be fine." Over at the ambulance, Johnny was shivering and his jacket was damp, but otherwise he appeared fairly bright. "He just needs to go to Ski Patrol for a check-up," Geoff continued, "then he can go home."

Mike spoke up. "I'll take him, if you like? Then I can deliver him to the school bus, assuming there's no problems?"

"Thanks, that'd be a help," nodded Geoff.

"No worries," said Mike. "See you back at the ski school," he called to Jude as he went over to shepherd Johnny to Ski Patrol.

Jude's attention switched back to Fiona, who was now lying prone on the trolley, cocooned in blankets and looking very small and white. She put a hand on Geoff's arm again. "How're *you* feeling?"

"Honestly?" His eyes were bright. "I'm worried sick. We haven't a clue what's wrong with her. It looks like concussion, but there's no obvious head injury."

"I'm sure the hospital will sort her out. Don't worry. That's the best place for her."

"I guess it could've been a lot worse." He grimaced. "That wee boy probably owes his life to Fiona. If she hadn't found him and got him up off the cliff we mightn't have found either of them."

Jude blinked in surprise. "But I thought she was scared of heights?"

Geoff's eyes widened. "Oh! I'd forgotten that." He stared over at the ambulance, where they were loading Fiona into the back, then gave the tiniest nod. One of the paramedics waved him over, and, as he turned to go, his words were so quiet that Jude only just caught them. "Maybe she was just more scared of losing another one."

Chapter 15

O N THE BACK SEAT of the Beechfields school bus, Amanda was pretending to be engrossed in the view from the window, ignoring the condensation that clouded the cold surface.

This time it was Johnny who was the centre of attention, and she was miffed that her so-called friends were hanging on his every word, rather than hanging around with her.

Still wearing the space blanket like a superhero cape, he was recounting his adventures, with the other children thronged around him. Even the teachers looked interested. "...and then she lifted me up over the edge. She's really strong. And really brave. I was a bit scared. And then she went unconscious, and I was even more scared, until the Ski Patrol yeti men arrived to help us." He looked down at the red scarf in his hands and said quietly, "I hope she's okay."

The tall instructor who'd accompanied Johnny back to the bus put a hand on the boy's shoulder. "I'm sure she'll be fine. Now," he glanced briefly at Mr Paton, "I need to get back to ski school, so I'll not take a lift down the road. See you next time." Lifting an arm in farewell, he disappeared out of the door.

With a sniff, Amanda turned back to the window. *She'd* fallen and got wet in the snow. But *she* hadn't needed rescuing, unlike Johnny. He was just a wimp, who was good at exaggerating and making the other children feel sorry for him. She tossed her hair off her shoulder. She would *never* do anything like that.

JUDE WATCHED the tail lights of the ambulance disappear through the snow like dying embers. With a sigh, she turned and made her way back to the ski school, trying to distract herself from worrying about Fiona by calculating whether they had enough instructors to cover classes tomorrow. Then the crunch of boots on snow alerted her to Mike loping across from the direction of the coach park.

"Alright?" he greeted her.

"I hope so. They've taken Fiona off to hospital. She's still unconscious."

"She'll be right. She's going to the best place."

She nodded, and went to open the hut door, but he put a gloved hand on top of hers.

"Leave it. Whatever it is, it can wait till tomorrow. Let's just lock up and you can take me home."

"Take you home?" She looked at him sideways.

He gave her a lopsided grin. "You know what I mean!"

She pursed her lips to stop them from curling into a smile.

"C'mon, it's late, gimme a break," he opened his hands, "I've missed the last bus and I need a lift."

She checked her watch. He was right, it *was* late. Lucy would be wondering where she'd got to. "Let me just switch the lights and heater off first." She unlocked the door.

He waited on the threshold. "I could treat you to dinner if you'd like? Save you being on your own tonight."

"Oh, I won't be on my own," she said as she bustled around making everything shipshape for tomorrow. "And I need to get back to Lucy, sorry."

He looked disappointed for a moment, and Jude suddenly realised that maybe *he* didn't want to be on his own that evening. "But you could come over for dinner later if you want? It won't be anything fancy, though. Especially if Lucy has started cooking."

He laughed at that. "Thanks, but I don't want to intrude on your family time. And I said I'd meet the others in the pub later. How about coffee tomorrow? My shout."

The worry flooded back. "If I don't need you to teach classes."

In two strides, he was across at the diary, and flipping the pages until he reached the correct date. Quickly, he scanned the entries as if memorising them. "Okay, I've got that. We can sort it out on the drive home. Now," he jerked a thumb over his shoulder at the door, "let's get out of here!"

Lucy sat at the kitchen table, a school jotter and glass of juice in front of her, see-sawing a pencil between two fingers. Homework was *boring*, but at least it was done, and now it was time to start on her play.

She was just contemplating whether she should use a pen name, or whether she'd mind being recognised in the street and asked for her autograph all the time, when she heard the front door bang. "Mum? Is that you?" It would be just her luck if it was a burglar. Although— would a burglar use the front door?

Jude came in, shaking the snow out of her hair. "Honey! I'm glad Sandy got you back alright." She planted a quick kiss on her daughter's cheek, and squeezed her shoulder. "It's great to see you. I've had a horrid day."

Lucy shrugged the hand off. "You think my day's been a bed of roses? Left waiting outside school like a lemon, getting frozen in the snow, and then having to put up with that Santa all the way home? He makes moaning into an art form."

Her mother sat down heavily. "Oh, honey, I'm sorry, I really am. But we did have an awful day."

"Yeah, right." She narrowed her eyes. "Dad would never have forgotten me!"

Jude's nostrils flared. "Your father..." she started, then shook her head quickly, and a flush rose up her neck. She took a breath. "I'm sorry, Lucy, everything went topsy turvy this afternoon. The blizzard came in whilst lessons were still on, and then Fiona went missing." She shook her head. "After everything she's been through, I couldn't bear to leave until I knew she was safe."

Fiona! Santa hadn't said that it was *her*. She liked Fiona. "What happened?"

"She went looking for one of her class. He'd fallen off the Ceann Mòr cornice, but Fiona managed to find him and get him back up the top." Jude sighed. "But she fell unconscious before Ski Patrol got there, and they had to rope her up the cliff and now they've taken her to hospital. Geoff was really worried."

Lucy liked Geoff too. He always reminded her of a bear. A friendly bear. And she knew her mother was friends with Fiona, maybe best friends, like she was with Ashlynn. *I would've been worried if Ashlynn had been lost in the blizzard.*

She picked up her pencil, and tapped it on her bottom lip. Maybe today's excuse for missing the school pick-up was a good one after all. Her eyes swivelled sideways. In which case she'd have to write her play about something else. Maybe 'Lost in a Blizzard'. Or 'The

Heroic Instructor'. Less avant-garde, but maybe more marketable? *Yes.* She'd get started on it tonight.

Standing up, Lucy put her arm around her mother and gave her a small hug. "I'm sorry, I hope she's alright. How did it happen?"

Chapter 16

FINGERS TAPPING AGAINST the collar of the ski jacket laid over his lap, Geoff sat on a plastic chair in the corridor outside a small, two-bedded side ward in the county hospital.

It felt like he'd been there forever. His nostrils itched with the sting of disinfectant and the cloying smell of flowers. He knew every word of every poster on the wall off by heart. He'd even started to recognise the staff by their footsteps alone. So when would they let him know what was going on with Fiona?

In the glass wall opposite, he noticed his distorted reflection. *You look like a scarecrow*, he thought. But then, was that a surprise? After the afternoon he'd had up the hill, searching for the love of his life in a blizzard, then the slippery ride down the hill in an ambulance clutching her small, cold, and now an evening spent worrying—

"Mr Easton, not to worry, just a little scare." A young doctor came out of the room and sat down beside him, clasping a clipboard in one hand and slotting a pen into the knot of hair at the back of her head with the other. "You can see her in a minute."

The tight band around Geoff's chest eased a little. He puffed out a breath. "So, what was wrong? Why was she unconscious?"

The doctor looked at him over her wire-rimmed glasses. "She's got Diabetes Mellitus." She had a bedside manner that could charitably be described as blunt.

Geoff blinked. "Diabetes? She can't have diabetes. She's fit as a fiddle."

The doctor ignored him. "It's often hidden—symptom-less—and only shows up when something like this happens." She pushed the specs up the bridge of her nose. "But the good news is, it's entirely treatable. In a day or two, once we've got her stable, we'll give her a machine to take home so she can check her blood glucose levels. With a little care and a careful diet, there's no reason she can't live an almost normal life."

Diabetes. Not what he'd expected to hear. And not good news. But—it would explain how she'd suddenly gone unconscious up the hill after the extra exertion of trying to save Johnny. And how they couldn't rouse her.

The doctor broke into his thoughts. "Now, we've given her some medication, and she's a lot brighter. Would you like to see her for ten minutes?"

WHEN MIKE PUSHED OPEN the heavy wooden door of The Rowan, he was assailed by the usual smell of woodsmoke, mingled with stale beer and pine cleanser. Over by the smouldering log fire, the other instructors were listening to Callum telling them some tall tale or other. Even Zoë was there—she'd obviously managed to rouse herself from her sick bed, and was looking surprisingly perky for someone who had supposedly been at death's door just a few hours earlier...

Unseen by them, Mike made his way over to the bar, with its ranks of malt whiskies and shelves stacked with glassware. The taciturn barman stepped closer, polishing a wine glass, and tilted his head at Mike. "The usual?"

In the corner, Callum's eyes were dancing as he regaled them with stories of today's Beechfields class. "...I tell you, I was lucky to get out of it alive. She might only have been fifteen, but she had all the moves. I think she'd have eaten me for breakfast!"

"And guess what he was today?" Debbie interjected. "A tightrope walker!"

Mike shook his head. "I think I'll have the cod and chips tonight. And just a water to drink." Order done, he strode over to join the others.

"At Blackpool Tower, don't forget that bit," added Callum. He stood up and did the mime. Then he remembered something else. "She's there for her summer holidays, she said. Blackpool. To see me, of course. But at least, if she eats me for breakfast," he paused for effect and wobbled, arms still outstretched, "she'll have a well-balanced meal!"

With a snort, Mike inserted himself into a spare chair beside Simon.

Debbie spotted him and waved in greeting. "Have you heard how Fiona is?"

At this, the others began to pepper him with enquiries after Fiona's health and questions about the rescue. He raised both hands. "One at a time!" Despite his worry, he felt a glow inside. It was nice to see how much they cared about their colleague. Succinctly, he told them about the rescue and how Fiona had helped the little boy. "We're just waiting to hear how she is. There's not been any news yet."

He sensed movement behind him, and turned to see the barman bearing down on them. "Your dinner." The dour man leaned over his shoulder and placed an over-flowing plate onto the table, along with cutlery and a tumbler of water.

"Thanks." Mike's stomach rumbled, and he tucked into the food as the clamour of noise and speculation roiled around him again. He'd almost finished—and the others had concluded that concussion was most likely—when his mobile phone started dancing around on the table beside him.

It was Jude. His throat constricted. *Would the news be good?* Pressing the green button, he put it to his ear, and everything went quiet around him. "She's okay," he heard, and raised a thumb at the others.

Relief washed over him—and them. She was going to be okay. *They* were going to be okay. His little band of instructors. And Jude. Her voice on the phone was melodious, like her personality, as she updated him on Fiona's condition. She was just *nice*, he realised. A good person. And one he wanted to be around more and more.

He glanced down at the wedding band on his left hand. Did that mean he was finally moving on? *Maybe.* But his heart had been frozen for a long time. So if it was going to thaw, it needed to be slowly. He was fine with that.

ZOË LOOKED up as the pub door swung open and her stomach gave a lurch. It was Ollie, wearing a vintage black Quiksilver top, baggy Fat Face trousers and that little half-smile that made her insides melt. Why did he have that effect on her?

Making that cupping, hand-rocking motion at her, he asked if she wanted a drink. She gave him a thumbs-up. A minute later, he was shuffling into the seat beside her and placing the two pints on the table in front of them. Then he moved closer so his thigh was pressed against hers, and nudged her with his hip. "How was your day?"

"Radical," she said, realising as she did so that the

surf-speak actually *did* describe her day pretty well. "And you?"

He lifted a shoulder. "Bit rubbish. The hill got closed so lessons finished early and I didn't get to do any free-riding."

"I heard."

"Was it one of your instructors that pushed a child off a cliff?" Ollie worked for *Snowbound*, one of the other ski schools.

Zoë frowned. "That's not actually what happened." It just showed you how gossip twisted things. Like the old lady being called 'Mad Meg' when she was actually just a bit confused and eccentric. "The boy had wandered away from his class and *fell* off the cliff. Then Fiona rescued him."

"Ah." Ollie lifted his pint and clinked it against hers. "I should've known Ed would have twisted things to make a better story."

"You were speaking to Ed?" Ed Griffiths was manager of *Ski-Easy*, another ski school in the valley.

"He gave me a lift, since the bus was full with everyone going down early. And then proceeded to pump me for information about our prices and lesson plans."

Zoë snorted. "That one always has an ulterior motive."

"Talking of which," Ollie put an arm around her shoulders and whispered in her ear, his breath sending shivers down her neck, "fancy coming back to mine again tonight?"

Around them, the hubbub of conversation from the other instructors rose and fell like waves on the sea. Nobody was listening to them. Nobody would judge her. But... "Would it be okay if I get a rain check on that? It's been a long day and I have to get up early tomorrow. I don't want to miss classes again."

For a moment he looked disappointed, but he quickly rallied. "No problem. Another time." Then he tilted his head at her. "So what did *you* get up to today, if it was such a long day? I didn't see you up the hill."

Zoë pressed her lips together, trying to formulate her thoughts. "I think I've worked out what I want to do in the summer. I met this old woman..."

She was half-way through telling him about Meg and the pottery lesson when her phone rang. The screen display said, 'Mother'. With a sigh, she said, "Sorry, I'd better get this."

"Zoë, darling," her mother's voice was tinny in her ear. And she sounded so *English*. *My ear must be getting attuned to all these Scots around me.* "I've got some terrible news. Uncle Louis has been taken into hospital—The Wellington. His cancer has flared up again, and they need to do some operation or other. The visiting hours are two to four every afternoon, and seven-thirty to nine in the evening."

Visiting hours? Did mother expect her to drop everything and go visit him? "Mother, I can't come down, I have classes every day. We're really busy here."

Ollie put a hand on her knee. "Do you need a lift somewhere?" he whispered. "I could take you."

In her ear, mother was saying, "I'm sure they could manage without you for a day. Your father could send a car."

"Hang on," she said into the phone, then put her palm over the microphone. "That's really sweet of you, Ollie, but she's talking about London. My uncle's in hospital."

"I could chum you," he said, a strand of black hair falling into his eyes and making him look like an Emo version of Keanu Reeves.

"Then both of us would be earning nothing."

He shrugged. "I've got my allowance."

"And I'm trying not to use mine."

The other shoulder lifted this time. "The offer's there if you want it."

Zoë turned back to the phone."Mother, I don't think I can get away. But I'll give you a phone tomorrow. Okay?"

Chapter 17
TUESDAY 10TH JANUARY

ZOE HADN'T SLEPT. But this time it wasn't Ollie's fault. She'd tossed and turned all night, feeling guilty about her uncle, until the grey light of dawn had crept around the curtains, and she decided she might as well get up.

A shower with her tangy lemon body wash had made her feel more human, and then a quick breakfast and the rattling bus journey into The Cairns, followed by a short, frosty walk on a sunny morning, had completed the job of waking her up.

She paused in front of Meg's front door, her hand on the tarnished brass knocker. Would the old dear even be up at this hour? And would she mind an early visit? After all, Zoë had said she'd come round *after* work, not before.

But coming now meant that she could keep her promise to the pensioner, do a morning's work at the ski school, travel to London in the afternoon, and hopefully get there just in time for evening visiting hour. Then she could get the sleeper back, and she'd only have missed an afternoon's work. It had all seemed quite plausible and sensible at four o'clock this morning, but in the harsh light of day—

"Yes?" The door swung open suddenly, and Meg stood there, leaning on her crutches. "Oh. It's you."

"Yes, sorry, I hope you don't mind. I'm going to be busy this afternoon so I thought I'd pop round this morning instead. Hope that's okay?"

The old woman grunted, but stood aside to let her in. "Tea?"

"Please." Zoë eyed up the bags of rubbish from last night's clearing session in the hall. "I'll just take these bags out to the bin, then we can get started in the lounge."

Two minutes later, Zoë had finished tidying the hall and had entered the sitting room, intending to make a start on the cluttered sideboard. But when Meg appeared from the kitchen, hopping on one crutch and clutching a mug of tea, she found her staring open-mouthed at photo in a smooth wooden frame.

"What?" The old woman demanded, placing the drink on an old shoe box at Zoë's elbow.

"This—" Zoë pointed at the photo of a small boy clutching the hand of a woman who looked like a younger version of Meg. "Who *is* this?"

"Let me see." Meg pushed her spectacles further up her nose, then she stilled. "Ah," she said, then shuffled to the other end of the sideboard and started poking in a box of Christmas tree baubles as if looking for treasure, and studiously ignoring Zoë's question.

"Is that you?" Zoë indicated the woman in the photo.

Her hands stilled. "Ye—es," she replied reluctantly.

"And the boy?"

She turned to face Zoë. "My son." This time she sounded defiant.

"You have a son?"

"Had."

Zoë blinked. "He died?"

The old lady's eyes became shuttered. "He's dead to me."

I need caffeine. This morning had totally gone topsy-turvy. Taking a gulp of her tea, Zoë looked from the photo to Meg, wondering if she was going mad. *Was* she seeing things? Because the boy in the photo looked like the spitting image of... "Was—is his name Louis?"

Meg staggered slightly and grabbed at the sideboard. "How did you know that?" Then she rallied, and her face hardened. "Have they been talking about me again? Blast those village gossips, have they nothing better to prattle about? Why would you listen to them?"

Her insides churning, Zoë rocked back on her heels. So it *was* Louis. It would explain a lot—why father hadn't wanted her to work here, why they'd never taken family holidays here, even though they often visited Scotland.

But it was still an earth-shattering coincidence. *My Uncle Louis is Meg's son.* Which meant that Meg... "I think you might be my great-aunt," she said slowly, pointing at the boy in the photo. "That's my Uncle Louis."

Leaning against the sideboard again, Meg stared at her. "Your uncle?"

"Louis Agnew. He runs a merchant bank in London. CEO. But, now that I think about it, I never met his parents. I think I heard that his mother had been ill, and I assumed she'd died..." Zoë trailed off. Meg's face had gone white as a sheet. "Are you okay? I think you should sit down."

With Meg safely installed in her armchair, Zoë went to the kitchen and quickly prepared another mug of tea, adding two sugars for good measure. "Here," she said, presenting it to the old woman. "But I thought your surname was Andrews?"

"Where did you hear that? I never told you that."

"No." Zoë wracked her brain. "I think it was the woman in the pharmacy."

"Pah. She never remembers me from one week to the next." She tapped a gnarly finger on the side of her forehead. "I'm Margaret Agnew. Always have been."

"So," From her perch on the settee, Zoë cradled her mug in both hands and leaned towards the old lady. "My Uncle Louis is your son." She still couldn't quite believe it. It was such a fluke that they'd even met. They wouldn't have, if it hadn't been for her drunken night with Ollie. "Can I ask, is his father still alive? Do I have a great-uncle as well?"

Meg shook her head. "He went back to France. Never

knew I was pregnant. I heard he'd died in an avalanche near Mont Blanc."

"So he was French. An instructor?"

The old woman nodded. "Could charm the birds from the trees. Jean-Claude Dufresne was his name."

They sat in silence for a minute. "You probably don't know then," Zoë said, twisting her hands in her lap, "there's some bad news about Uncle Louis. He's sick. Cancer. My mother actually phoned last night to say he's in hospital again."

Meg's watery eyes turned to Zoë, and a tear faltered down her wrinkled cheek.

It made Zoë want to cry too, something she never did. Was this what discovering long-lost relatives did? Did it make you into an emotional wreck? Blinking hard, she knelt beside the old woman and put an arm around her shoulder—something else she never normally did. "I'm sorry," she said gently. "But I have a suggestion."

THE SKY WAS the deepest azure blue and the morning sun made the snow sparkle like a sea of glass. Scottish mountain weather was like Jekyll and Hyde, Mike mused. Hell one day, heaven the next. It was literally the lull after the storm.

Waving goodbye to the private lesson pupil he'd just finished with, he propped his skis against the wall of the ski school hut, and went over to the café.

Five minutes later, he clomped back up the steps clutching two takeaway cups. Inside, all was quiet as the main classes had started for the day and all the other instructors were out. "I brought you coffee."

Jude had been sitting at the counter, concentrating on some paperwork. She sat up and stretched, "Oh *yes*, thanks, that's exactly what I need. I was starting to drift off."

Putting his peppermint tea on the table, Mike busied himself taking off his boots. "Has Geoff been in touch?"

"Yes," Jude replied, "they're keeping her in for another day or so to monitor her condition and carry out more tests."

"Right." He nodded thoughtfully. "At least they know what it is now." He hung his jacket on a peg. "And it's treatable."

"Yes. Better to know, I always think."

That stopped him in his tracks. *She* used to say that too.

Jude caught sight of his face. "Mike?" she frowned. "Are you okay?"

"Yeah, she'll be right." But he wasn't alright. He sat down, his shoulders slumped. "Sometimes you remind me of her." He looked at her from under his eyebrows. "Not to look at, just things you say now and again."

She put a hand on his arm. "Your wife?"

"I miss her so much." He touched the ring on his left hand and sighed. "But it's been ages. I should be over it, by now."

"And you think you are. And then something comes along, and 'bang!', it brings it all back, just like it was yesterday." She spun round and went to stare out of the window.

Slowly, Mike stood, and then joined her at the window. A sheen of cirrus clouds high in the atmosphere heralded a change in the weather—the 'Hyde' part that he'd been thinking about earlier. He gave Jude a sideways look. "Your husband?"

"Yes." She bit her lip and hesitated before continuing in a rush. "I'm scared he's not coming back."

He nodded. That would probably explain why she sometimes seemed so lacking in confidence. But she'd done well, to get everything going for the season given how little experience she had. Reaching across, he put a hand on top of hers, which felt small and delicate in comparison to his. "Don't worry, I'm sure he'll be back soon." He gestured at the view out of the window and quirked a lip. "How could he resist this wonderful Scottish weather?"

But he knew that she remembered yesterday's blizzard just as well as he did. *Jekyll and Hyde.* And which was this husband of hers? Was he a well-meaning father who'd gone to New Zealand to raise money for his family, or a good-for-nothing drongo who'd abandoned his wife and child and had no intention of coming back?

Time would tell. And he had plenty of that.

❄

THE NEXT AFTERNOON, Fiona sat in her hospital bed, listening to music on her iPod and flicking through a skiing magazine. After a morning full of tests and examinations by an endless succession of medics in white lab coats, she was glad of a little bit of peace.

There was a tentative knock on the door, and she looked up to see little Johnny peeking round the door. "Can I come in, Miss?"

She nodded, smiling broadly as she removed the earbuds. "I'm so glad to see you!"

As the door opened wider and Johnny came towards her, she spotted Mr Paton lurking in the corridor, pulling his phone out of his pocket.

Johnny hovered awkwardly until she motioned him to a chair. She had to hide a smile when she noticed that his blazer was mis-buttoned and one of his shoelaces was trailing. *You'd think the teacher would've sorted him out.* The staff at Beechfields obviously didn't do motherly stuff.

The boy sat down, darting glances around the room, then pulled off his scarf and clasped it in his lap. "How are you, Miss? I was really worried about you, and I made them let me come to visit you."

"Oh, I'm fine, now. And it's really nice of you to worry about me. I was worried about you, too. I'm really pleased that you're okay."

He fiddled with his scarf, his cheeks turning pink.

"I couldn't have done it without you, you know," she added softly, "I'd have given up, on my own."

He looked up, a flash of understanding in his face. "But I helped you be like Robert the Bruce?"

She nodded. "Yes, I guess you did."

He stood up, and went over to her locker, where flowers and 'Get Well' missives fought for attention. "You've got a lot of cards." He touched one with a colourful toucan on the front.

They were interrupted by a rap on the door, and Mr Paton stepped in. He cleared his throat. "Johnny, we need to get back now. Say goodbye, and then meet me by the reception desk."

As the door closed behind the teacher, Johnny turned back to her. He opened his mouth, but no words came out. Then, with a quick glance across at the flowers, he stepped to the bed and put his scarf into her hands. He found the words. "Here, Miss, have my scarf, it'll help you remember about being brave. Like Robert..."

"...the Bruce?" She finished for him, smiling.

"Yes!" He smiled back.

"Before you go," she motioned him closer, "let me fix your buttons." He stood patiently whilst she righted his blazer, then patted his chest. "And one of your laces is undone."

He looked down in surprise, and ducked almost out of sight whilst he re-tied it. "Thanks, Miss," he said when he stood up, then paused awkwardly and wriggled his shoulders.

She held out her arms. "D'you want a wee hug?"

He smelled of toothpaste and apples, and hugged more fiercely than she expected, taking her breath away.

"Goodbye, Miss," he said as he broke away and turned for the door.

"'Bye, Johnny," she replied. "See you next ski lesson?"

He turned and grinned at her, his face sparkling, and then he was gone.

Fiona pursed her lips, and looked down at the scarf in her lap. After a moment, she folded it carefully and placed it on the locker beside her other gifts.

"I'LL LEAVE YOU TO IT." Zoë crept past Meg, who was clutching her son's hand and murmuring softly to him.

Louis' face against the cotton pillow was grey and drawn, and his hand on the white sheet was thin and bony. He was only a shadow of the hearty, blustering man Zoë remembered from her youth. But he seemed to have rallied somewhat when they arrived at his bedside and he realised who Meg was.

"So he didn't mind?" Ollie peered around the door jamb. The private room in the fancy hospital was all navy and chrome—it was only the utilitarian bed and undertone of disinfectant that signalled you were in a medical establishment rather than an upmarket business institute. But maybe the neutral setting helped to reduce stress? No doubt there'd been some expensive research behind the interior design decisions.

Zoë shook her head as she joined Ollie in the corridor. "I think he was pleased to see her." And she'd been secretly pleased when Ollie had found out what she was planning, and insisted he came with them to London. He'd been good company on the train down, and had helped to draw Meg out, eliciting stories of past ski exploits and long-gone colleagues.

He was good for the old dear, who had blossomed under his attentions. *And maybe good for me too,* she realised. But if Zoë wanted to make this relationship last, she was determined to learn from Meg's mistake, and take things slowly for a change. If Ollie was worth it, and if what they had together was real, he'd understand.

"I think we've got time for a quick coffee before we have to head back to the station," she said, spotting a sign that pointed to the cafeteria.

"Great," he said, reaching for her hand. "I wanted to chat to you about the summer."

Warmth blossomed in Zoë's insides, and she couldn't help but smile. *I think he's worth it.*

Chapter 18
WEDNESDAY 11TH JANUARY

Geoff poked at the glucose-testing machine, trying to guess how it worked. "So how do you use this thing?"

Fiona looked up from where she'd been cutting the hospital ID band off her wrist. She put the scissors down and came to join him at the dining table. "I use the pinprick thing to get a drop of blood, and put it in there," she pointed, "and then it gives a reading. And that lets me know if I need medication, or if I need to eat something."

"Amazing," he looked up at her. "Let me know if I can help you with it. Remind you or whatever... anything."

She took his hand, and looked into his eyes. "They told me something interesting—important—at the hospital today."

He wrinkled his forehead. "Uh-huh?"

"They said that if I can keep my glucose levels steady, I should be able to carry a baby to full term." She paused and dropped her eyes. "That's probably been the problem the last two times. We just didn't know."

Geoff frowned. "Would you really want to risk it? I thought you were too scared to try again?"

She moved behind him and put her arms around his shoulders. "I learned something yesterday, from little Johnny. He said not to give up." Geoff twisted round to look at her. "And I didn't. And we were okay." She kissed the tip of his nose. "I think he's right. We shouldn't give up. We should try again." A smile broke out across her face. "Some of them are worth the risk."

Hope surged in Geoff's chest. Wouldn't it be ironic if it had taken an accident to fix things between them? He stood up and pulled her closer.

"Let's try again, Geoff."

"Are you sure?" He looked for confirmation in her eyes.

"Totally." Then she took him by the hand and led him up the stairs to bed...

EPILOGUE

MONIQUE CARSON tapped an acrylic nail on her ruby-red bottom lip. Why did Orson always make it so difficult any time she asked for time off? She just wanted to learn to ski, so that next time there was a royal holiday to cover, she'd get first dibs. "Well, if you really must, I *suppose* I could maybe work an article into my trip."

From behind his massive solid oak statement desk, her editor carefully folded up his shirt sleeves, looking at her over the top of his rimless glasses. "Something that'll appeal to the forty-something divorcée crowd. That's the demographic that Marketing say read your column."

Clenching her jaw, she glared at him. She was sure he did it deliberately, the old queen, reminding her at every opportunity of how Felix had tossed her aside like yesterday's trash, and moved on to a younger model. Literally. Although Monique was sure that the height of Penelope's career had been catalogue shoots. Surely that scheming tramp wasn't tall enough for runway.

But that gave her an idea, something that she could rub in Felix's face and would give him a taste of his own medicine. "How about... The Hunt for a Younger Model: Finding a Toyboy in the Highlands of Scotland."

Orson's eyes stared sideways for a moment, as if thinking. Then his face cleared. "Finding a Toyboy in the Après Ski Capital of Scotland," he said decisively.

He always has to better my ideas. But she liked the idea of après ski. That was half the point of skiing, wasn't it? And snowsports resorts would be full of young, fit, handsome men with plenty of energy and good conversation. She could see it now, swooping down the slopes, laughing with a gorgeous bronzed instructor, then cuddling up beside him at night in front of a roaring log fire...

"Two weeks," Frank slapped his desk. "Two weeks, and then I want the copy. Bring me scandal and scuttlebutt. Bring me cheating and backstabbing. We didn't make *Tattle* the bestselling gossip magazine in the UK by pussyfooting around with social niceties. Tell it like it is. Warts and all."

"Right," she said, smoothing down the skirt of her Bella Freud suit and smothering a frisson of excitement as she stalked out of his office and sashayed through the open plan office. Two weeks in the Scottish Highlands, learning to ski and finding a younger man to fall in love with her. That should be fun.

Then she caught some delivery guy giving her a

second glance as he placed a box on a secretary's desk. He was tall, with Mediterranean good looks and bulging biceps. Probably from all the lifting. Maybe... But then she stopped herself. *Blue collar.* Not worth her time.

However, his attention proved something: *I still have it*. Regular gym sessions and careful eating had kept her in the same dress size that she'd worn at twenty-one. And she had a wonderful hairdresser and a miracle-working beautician. *Those Scottish hunks won't know what's hit them.*

Reaching her desk, she grabbed the phone. She'd get her assistant to make the reservations right away, before Orson changed his mind. Now, what was the name of that ski school, the one with the 'learn to ski in a week' offer? *Ah yes, White Cairns, that was it!*

What happens next? *Find out by reading the next episode:*

Buy *My Snowy Valentine*

A NOTE FROM THE AUTHOR

Thank you for reading, and I really hope you enjoyed the story. If so, please take a moment to **leave a review** and tell a friend!

The *Secrets in the Snow* series is based on experiences I had whilst working for a number of ski schools in Scotland.

Bad weather, awkward pupils and eccentric locals are not always just figments of my imagination—for example, Meg is based on an old lady I used to see up the mountain in her centuries-old ski suit, and also pushing her bike around the streets of Aviemore. I'm sure the lifties were all scared of her and that she never had to buy a ski pass! But other than that, I know nothing of her story—so I made it up!

The series

As the season progresses in *Secrets in the Snow*, we'll get to know the other instructors better, and learn more about their stories. In the next book, *My Snowy Valentine*, we'll discover more about Mike, the chief instructor, and his background in New Zealand.

The series prequel, *Winter Arrives*, which introduces the characters and tells of how Jude took over the ski school, can be yours **free**, just for signing up to my mailing list: rozmarshall.co.uk/welcome/

Read on for an extract from *My Snowy Valentine*.

Hope to see you again soon!

AN EXTRACT FROM MY SNOWY VALENTINE

SECRETS IN THE SNOW, EPISODE 3

"I'm VERY SORRY to do this to you, Mike," said the older man, "you know I wouldn't ask unless I had to."

Based on Sandy's past form, like turfing him out for Christmas Day, Mike wasn't so sure.

"But we've had these bookings for ages," continued Sandy, "and, to be honest, when you arrived at the door last year, I thought you'd only stay for a night or two so it wouldn't be an issue. But it's been, what, two months now?"

"Yeah, near enough," agreed Mike.

"It's because it's half-term; we're always full in the school holidays. It's the same at Easter," said Sandy. "Jean and I are run off our feet—especially since I have to leave for work at the ski school after breakfast and she has to do all the rooms herself."

Mike nodded. "I'll find something else, she'll be right."

"You'll be okay till Thursday the ninth, but we've a full house from Friday." Sandy puffed out his chest. When he did that, he looked more like Father Christmas than ever, with his grey-white beard and rosy cheeks. *It's no wonder the others call him Santa when he's not in earshot.* "For two weeks," Sandy continued, "two and a bit, actually, if you include the weekends." He leaned in conspiratorially. "Different schools choose different weeks for half-term. So it lasts for longer."

Mike nodded again. So he needed to find somewhere to stay for over two weeks, during one of the busiest winter periods. And he needed access to the internet, which he'd discovered was quite unusual in this rural backwater. He sighed inwardly. Maybe it was time to think about moving on.

"No worries," he told Sandy.

But he *would* worry. He'd just learned to keep his worries to himself.

AS MIKE CROSSED the village street, ski boots dangling by their straps in his gloved hands, Jude was juggling a large box and a bunch of keys as she struggled to open the door of the ski school shop. "Morning, boss," he greeted her.

She turned at his voice and tutted at him as she pushed the door open. "Please don't call me that!" she chided. "You know Allan's really the boss."

He followed her into the shop, picking up a pile of envelopes from the doormat as he passed. "But Allan's in New Zealand. And you're running things here. Anyway, it's *your* ski school, isn't it? Didn't you tell me your dad left it to you?"

"Well, yes," she admitted grudgingly as she put the box on the counter. "But 'boss' just sounds so..." she paused and pursed her lips, searching for the right word, "*formal*, I suppose. I still feel like an impostor, most of the time."

He handed her the letters. "But you're doing a great job—you won that new contract from Beechfields. And the 'ski with Santa' thing at Christmas went down well with the kids, didn't it?"

She made a face. "Yes, but not so well with all the instructors!"

Laughing, he remembered Sandy stomping off across the car park in his red Santa outfit. "Yeah, but Sandy's *never* happy. It makes his day to have something to complain about!"

"Actually, I was meaning Zoë. It *seriously* undermined her street cred, having to wear that fake beard."

He raised his eyebrows. "Might have taught her some humility, perhaps? Maybe you did her a favour."

She smiled, and riffled through the envelopes in her hand, stopping at one made from an expensive-looking cream vellum. "Ski Development Trust? I wonder who they are?" she asked rhetorically, and put the rest of the pile on the counter, picking up a letter-opener.

She was quiet for a moment as she scanned the contents of the letter. Then her hand went to her mouth. "Oh!" She looked up at him. "They want us to run some ski trials for them. To find candidates for their race training programme. And then run the race training for them. One of their kids was in our Santa classes at Christmas and recommended us."

"That's good, isn't it?"

"Well, yes, but I don't think we can. Do the racing thing, I mean."

"Why not? There's plenty of slalom poles."

"Yes, but we don't have any timing equipment. We've never needed it."

He shrugged. "We should just buy some, then."

She shook her head. "No, we've not enough money for that."

He frowned. "But—"

"I know you said we're doing well. But Al—," she corrected herself, "but the ski school was struggling somewhat last year, and we're still recovering, financially. So I'm afraid there's no spare money for equipment."

"Maybe you could borrow the kit?"

She raised her chin and looked upwards as she thought it over. "The only timing kit I know of belongs to *Ski-Easy*. But I don't think they'd loan it to us. They'd want the contract themselves."

He nodded slowly. He'd met Ed Griffiths, the manager of their rival ski school, and had privately thought that he was the sort of man who got Scots a reputation for meanness. "What about hiring, then?"

She rubbed her lip, then nodded, "Yes, I'll look into that. There must be somewhere." Then she looked up at the clock on the wall above the door. "We'd better get up the hill. Classes start soon!"

Half an hour later, they arrived up the hill at the ski school hut. "Oh, what's that?" Jude nodded at the door, as their boots crunched on the new snow that dusted the steps.

Mike pulled the flyer out of the letterbox as Jude unlocked the door. "Ski School Race," he said, skim-reading the text. "A tie-in with the Winter Olympics. Wednesday the fifteenth. Ski and snowboard teams. Ah!" He stopped short as they stepped into the hut.

She turned back and looked at him quizzically. "What's the problem?"

"Not a problem, it's the first prize." He grinned at her. "It's race equipment!"

Her eyes widened. "Oh!" She started to smile, but then a troubled look crossed her face. "But we'd need to win." She frowned. "Could we win?" she asked him.

"We could have a pretty good try. After all, we've got Ben, which will give us an advantage. I could start some Race Training with the others."

"Racing?" said a male voice behind them. "Annual Ski

School Race, Ben," Mike said, turning to the fair-haired young man who'd just entered, and handing him the flyer. "We're hoping your British Team expertise might help us!"

"I'll leave the racing to you youngsters," said Sandy, stroking his silvery beard. "I believe my slalom days are well and truly over." He turned to Mike, raising a palm magnanimously. "However, put me down as a substitute, if you need one."

Mike nodded. "Come along to the training, though, Sandy, just in case." He looked round at the others, who were gazing expectantly at him from various perches around the ski school hut. "But I'll need *all* of the rest of you." He looked over at a lanky guy who was sprawled untidily over one of the pine chairs. "And Simon, I think I'll need you in both teams—boarding and skiing— unless Sandy skis after all." He grimaced. "And I'm still short of a lady for the snowboard team."

"There's no 'I' in team," muttered Callum, who was usually the joker of the pack.

Mike looked sideways at him, waiting for the punch-line, but none was forthcoming. He raised his eyebrows. "Right, *we* still need a second lady for the snowboard team."

"Is there an age limit?" asked Jude.

Mike's brow furrowed. "I thought you didn't ski—or board?" He noticed Fiona shooting Jude a look.

"Oh, not me, I meant Lucy," Jude said, flustered, "she's quite good on a board."

"But Lucy's not an instructor," said Fiona. "I think the racers need to be instructors?"

Mike rubbed his temple whilst he contemplated that.

"Perhaps she could 'work' for us next weekend—as a part-time trainee. That would make her count as an 'instructor', wouldn't it?" suggested Zoë.

"But wouldn't it be a bit dishonest?" said Debbie, screwing up her nose.

Sandy made a 'harumph' sound. "I'll bet that wouldn't stop *Ski-Easy* from filling their team with shills and ringers if they thought that would help them win."

"No need to do anything like that," interjected Ben, waving the the race flyer above his head theatrically. "One of the rules says you can co-opt a relative or neighbour into the team. And it's anyone over the age of twelve. So Lucy would count."

Jude beamed a smile at him. "That's wonderful!"

Mike looked across at Jude. "Would you be able to get her up here after school so she could do race training with us?"

She nodded. "I'm sure we could work something out." She turned to the rest of the group. "Can I just say 'thank-you' to all of you for agreeing to do this? Obviously it's good to get our name out there and there will be some prestige if we win; but the first prize of race equipment would be really useful as it would let me accept a new contract with the Ski Development Trust to run race training and trials—which would obviously provide more work for some of you." She smiled at them.

Ben cleared his throat, and pointed at the leaflet again. "There's an incentive for *us*, as well." He got some curious glances. "Members of the winning team also get *Sports Market* vouchers. So there's even more reason to win."

"Well, hopefully with you on our team, Ben, we'll have a great chance of doing just that!" said Jude. "But just do your best, everyone."

"Okay," Mike looked round at them all, "that's us sorted then. From now on we'll meet at the top of the Creag Dheighe for race training every night as soon as you're finished with your classes." Then he glanced up at the clock. "Talking of which—time to rattle your dags— lessons start soon. I'll see you out there!"

Linda, the ski area administrator, smiled up at him from under her fringe. "Mornin', Mike. Are you here to enter Winters' into the ski school race?"

"Er, yeah," replied Mike, and pushed the forms across her desk. He'd just about got used to locals calling the ski school Winters' after its owners, rather than its proper name of 'White Cairns Ski School'.

"Don't know why you're bothering," drawled a voice

from the doorway. Mike turned and saw a pony-tailed bloke with teeth like tombstones and dissolute, droopy eyes, wearing the fluorescent-green jacket of *Ski-Easy*, their rival ski school.

Linda smiled politely at the new arrival and said, "Well, good morning to you too, Ed. So are you here to enter the ski school race an' all?"

He slapped a couple of entry forms onto Linda's desk, then turned to Mike, turning up the collar of his jacket and squaring his shoulders as he did so. "We're going to walk it. I reckon we could win even if we tied our hands behind our backs and skied blindfolded."

Gamesmanship or delusion? Mike looked Ed in the eye and decided it was the former. He raised his eyebrows.

Before he had time to reply, Linda intervened. "Yer man Ben Dalton works for you, Mike, doesn't he?" she asked, innocently.

He turned back to her. "Yeah."

"Sure, but he'll give you an advantage in the race, won't he?"

"Advantage? What advantage?" blustered Ed.

Linda's eyes took on a dreamy, unfocussed look. "I used to watch him on 'Ski Sunday'. It's a crying shame he had that accident last year—we might have been cheering him on in the Winter Olympics otherwise." She gave her head an imperceptible shake, as if to clear an unwelcome image.

Ed's brow furrowed, and he turned to Mike. "That

can't be right. You're not allowed to have Olympic skiers in your team!"

Mike shrugged. "He works for our ski school. Has done since December. I'm surprised you hadn't heard," he replied evenly.

"Huh. Well, one skier doesn't make a ski team." Ed's eyes narrowed. "As they say, 'no man is an island; everyone is a part of a continent'," he misquoted, and flicked a hand dismissively. "We'll soon see if the rest of you match up to your star player." He turned on his heel and stomped out.

Linda slapped her palms down on her desk. "Well, *that* went well, didn't it now?" she said, and smiled mischievously. "I can't help but mess with that guy, he's such a *gobshite,* so he is!"

Her accent made the expletive sound like something Gollum would've said in 'The Lord of the Rings', and Mike found himself grinning at her. "You'll get me into trouble!"

If only he'd realised how prescient that was…

If you liked this extract, you can buy the full novella on most eBook stores:

Buy *My Snowy Valentine*

OTHER BOOKS IN THE SERIES

The *Secrets in the Snow* books, in chronological order:

Prequel, *"Winter Arrives"*

Short Story 1, *"Skiing with Santa"*

Short Story 2, "*A Dream for New Year*"

Book I, "*Fear of Falling*"

Short Story 3, "*The Snow Patrol*"

Book 2, "*My Snowy Valentine*"

Book 3, "*The Racer Trials*"

Book 4, "*Snow Blind*"

Book 5, *"Weathering the Storm"* completes the series

Paperback *"Secrets in the Snow, The Complete Season"*, contains Books 0-5 and Short Stories 1-3.

ABOUT THE AUTHOR

Roz lives in Scotland with her husband and the obligatory dog and cat. Her writing experience includes screenwriting, songwriting, web pages and even sentiments for greeting cards!

I also write in other genres:

Cozy Mysteries, as R.B. Marshall: books2read.com/rl/RBMarshall

Historical Romance, telling the story of Mary Queen of Scots, as Belle McInnes: books2read.com/rl/MarysLadies

Here's where you'll find me:
rozmarshall.co.uk/books

ALSO BY ROZ MARSHALL

*The **Celtic Fey** series*

Urban Fantasy / Young Adult Fantasy set in Scotland (and the faerie realm):

- Unicorn Magic
- Kelpie Curse
- Faerie Quest
- The Fey Bard
- Merlin's Army (due in 2020)
- The Celtic Fey (Books 1-3. Also in paperback)

Half Way Home stories

Young Adult Science Fiction set in Hugh Howey's *Half Way Home* universe.

- Nobody's Hero
- The Final Solution

Scottish stories:

- Still Waters

Writing as R.B. Marshall:

*The **Highland Horse Whisperer** series*

Cozy Mystery set in Scotland (and London for the prequel):

- The Secret Santa Mystery
- A Corpse at the Castle
- A Right Royal Revenge (releasing 30 Sept 2020)
- A Henchman at the Highland Games (due in 2021)

Writing as Belle McInnes:

Mary's Ladies

Scottish Historical Romance telling the story of Mary Queen of Scots:

- *A Love Divided*
- *A Love Beyond*
- *A Love Concealed (releasing 31 Aug 2020)*

GLOSSARY

Abseil: Moving down a steep incline by means of ropes secured above and placed around the body, and paid out gradually in the descent

Belay: Secure a rope by attaching to a person or to an object offering stable support

Blue collar: Manual worker

Cakehole: slang for mouth

Cornice: Lip of snow projecting over a mountain ridge

First dibs: First chance, be first choice

Free-riding: Snowboarding or skiing combining multiple styles and terrains, such as jumps, half-pipes and obstacles

Ikea: Furniture and homeware store

Liftie: Ski lift operator

Messages: Scots expression for groceries, shopping

Parallel (skiing): Advanced skiing method

P.E.: Physical Education

Pinny: Apron

Piste: A ski slope

Robert the Bruce: Legendary Scottish king who gained inspiration from watching a spider build its web

Ski Patrol: Organisation responsible for safety at a ski resort

Snowplough: Beginner ski movement

Wally: Idiot

Whiteboard: White plastic marker board

CHARACTERS

Allan (Winters): Jude's husband
Amanda: Ski pupil
Ben Dalton: Ski instructor
Callum Johnstone: Ski instructor
Davie: Ski lift operator
Debbie McNeill: Ski instructor
Fiona Easton: Ski instructor; Geoff's wife
Forbes Sinclair: Ski area operations manager
Geoff Easton: Ski patroller; Fiona's husband
Mr (James) **Paton**: Head of PE, *Beechfields School*
Johnny: Ski pupil
Jude Winters: Acting manager, *White Cairns Ski School*
Louis Agnew: Zoë's uncle
Lucy (Winters): Jude and Allan's daughter
Marty Ferguson: Snowboard instructor
Meg: Resident of The Cairns
Mike Cole: *White Cairns'* chief instructor

Monique Carson: Journalist

Natalie: Ski pupil

Ollie: *Snowbound* ski instructor

Orson: Editor of *Tattle* magazine

Sandy Potter (Santa): Ski instructor

Simon Jones (Spock): Ski/snowboard instructor

Zoë Agnew: Snowboard instructor

ACKNOWLEDGMENTS

Thank you to Andrea, Mairi, Angie and Debbie, my beta-reading and editing team, who added extra polish and value to my scribblings. Also thanks to Claire for her brainstorming ideas. Much appreciated!

Printed in Great Britain
by Amazon